Mike & Coinga,

Happy retirement and a big thank you for your support over the years! You two are AWESOME!

[signature]
9/3/22

White Spider Night

The *Emerson Moore* Adventures by Bob Adamov

- *Rainbow's End* — Released October 2002
- *Pierce the Veil* — Released May 2004
- *When Rainbows Walk* — Released June 2005
- *Promised Land* — Released July 2006
- *The Other Side of Hell* — Released June 2008
- *Tan Lines* — Released June 2010
- *Sandustee* — Released March 2013
- *Zenobia* — Released May 2014
- *Missing* — Released April 2015
- *Golden Torpedo* — Released July 2017
- *Chincoteague Calm* — Released April 2018
- *Flight* — Released May 2019
- *Assateague Dark* — Released May 2020
- *Sunset Blues* — Released April 2022

The *Zeke Layne* Adventure by Bob Adamov

Memory Layne — Released May 2021

Next *Emerson Moore* Adventure:
Rainbow's End
20th Anniversary Edition

White Spider Night

Bob Adamov

Packard Island Publishing
Wooster, Ohio
2022
www.packardislandpublishing.com
www.bobadamov.com

Copyright 2022 by Bob Adamov
All rights reserved. No part of this book may be used or reproduced in any manner whatsoever without written permission from the author except in the case of brief quotations embodied in critical articles or reviews.

www.BobAdamov.com

This book is a work of fiction. Names, characters, places and incidents are either products of the author's imagination or are used fictitiously. Any resemblance to actual events, locales or persons, living or dead, is entirely coincidental.

First edition • July 2022

ISBN: 979-8-9853593-1-2

Library of Congress Number: 2022907675

Printed and bound in the United States of America

Cover art by: Ryan Sigler
Blue River Digital
303 Towerview Dr.
Columbia City, IN 46725
www.blueriverd.com

Printed by:
Bookmasters, Inc.
PO Box 388
Ashland, OH 44805
www.Bookmasters.com

Layout design by: Ryan Sigler
Blue River Digital
303 Towerview Dr.
Columbia City, IN 46725
www.blueriverd.com

Published by:
Packard Island Publishing
3025 Evergreen Drive
Wooster, OH 44691
www.packardislandpublishing.com

Dedication

This book is dedicated to my dear friend Tom Ohlemacher who passed away in January 2022. Over several days, I was focused on the final edit of the previous novel *Sunset Blues* and seeing Tom Ohlemacher's name repeatedly in the manuscript as he was featured in it. You can imagine my shock upon hearing the news of his passing!

I will miss you, my dear friend! We met when you bought a copy of my first book *Rainbow's End*. We connected so well and you helped me with island background information – and you encouraged me to continue writing. Your stories were outrageously funny, especially about the Duck Factory and finding stolen Put-in-Bay street signs on Grosse Ile.

I placed you in a couple of scenes in my second book *Pierce the Veil* after you coached me with a scene at Perry's Monument. I always looked forward to our visits and, in the last years, to our phone conversations.

You were helping me with *Sunset Blues* in which you appear as the Put-in-Bay police chief. You were excited about playing a major role, leading an island murder investigation, in *White Spider Night*. Rest in peace. We all miss you!

They that wait upon the Lord shall renew their strength;
they shall mount up with wings as eagles;
they shall run, and not be weary;
and they shall walk, and not faint.
        – Isaiah 40:31

Acknowledgments

For technical assistance, I'd like to express my appreciation to Dave Nostrant, Michael Gora, Bill Lodermeier, Bob Schneider, Eddie Sheller, Clay Cozart, Cory Sipert, Mark Wilhelm, Joe Burke, Tom Ohlemacher, Bob Gatewood, and Roger Chester.

I'd like to thank my senior editor John Wisse and my team of editors: Cathy Adamov and Michelle Marchese plus proof reader Doreen Chester. An additional thank you to John Wisse for his editorial comments that changed the first chapter's opening scene, making it more dynamic.

For more information, check these sites:
BobAdamov.com
VisitPut-in-Bay.com
MillerFerry.com

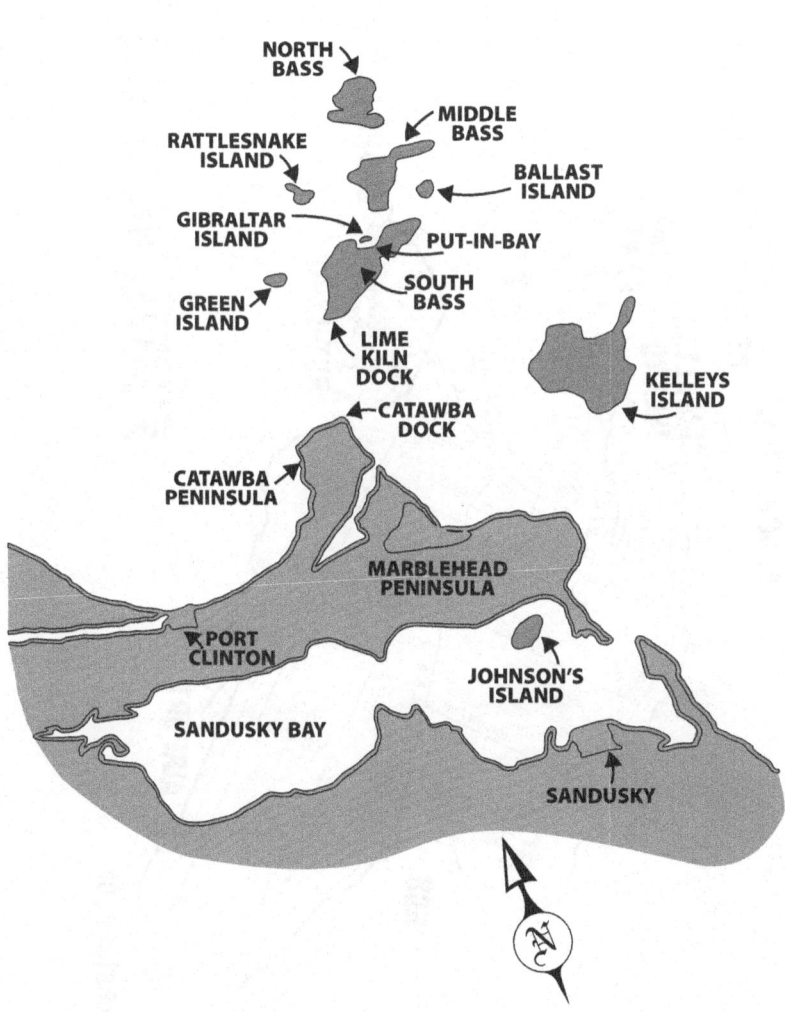

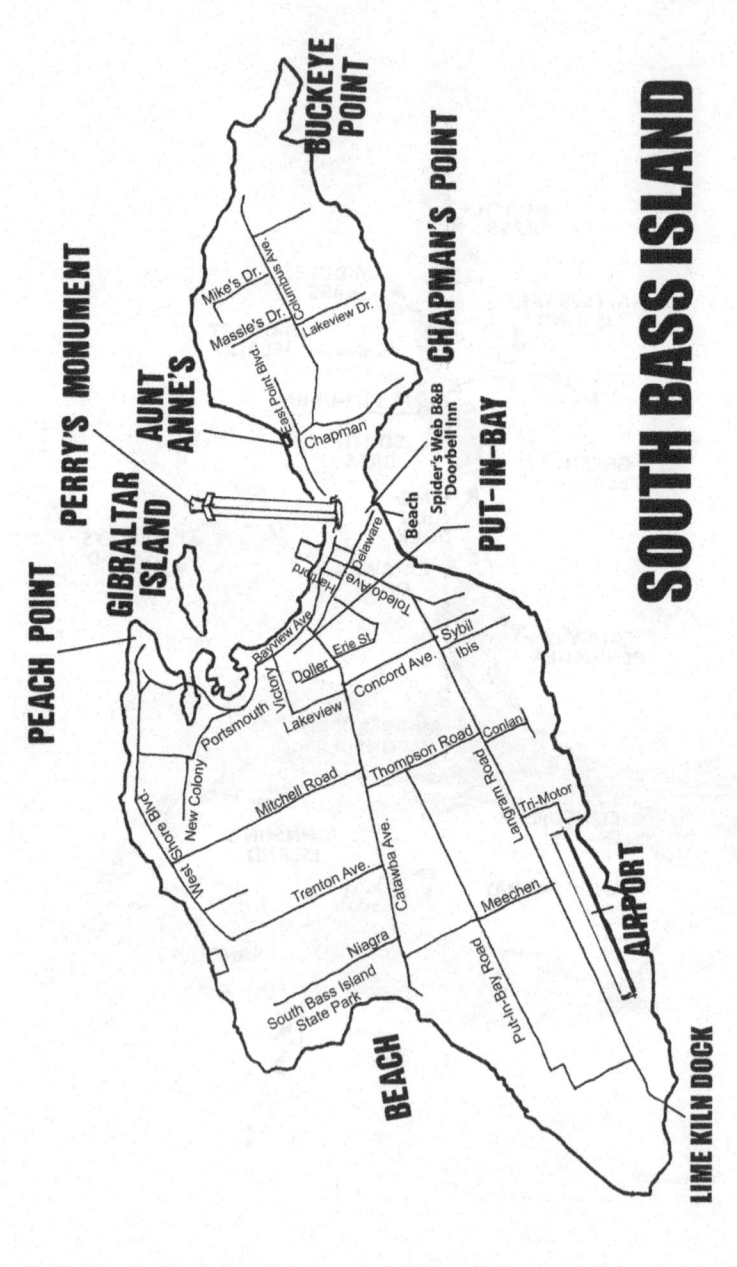

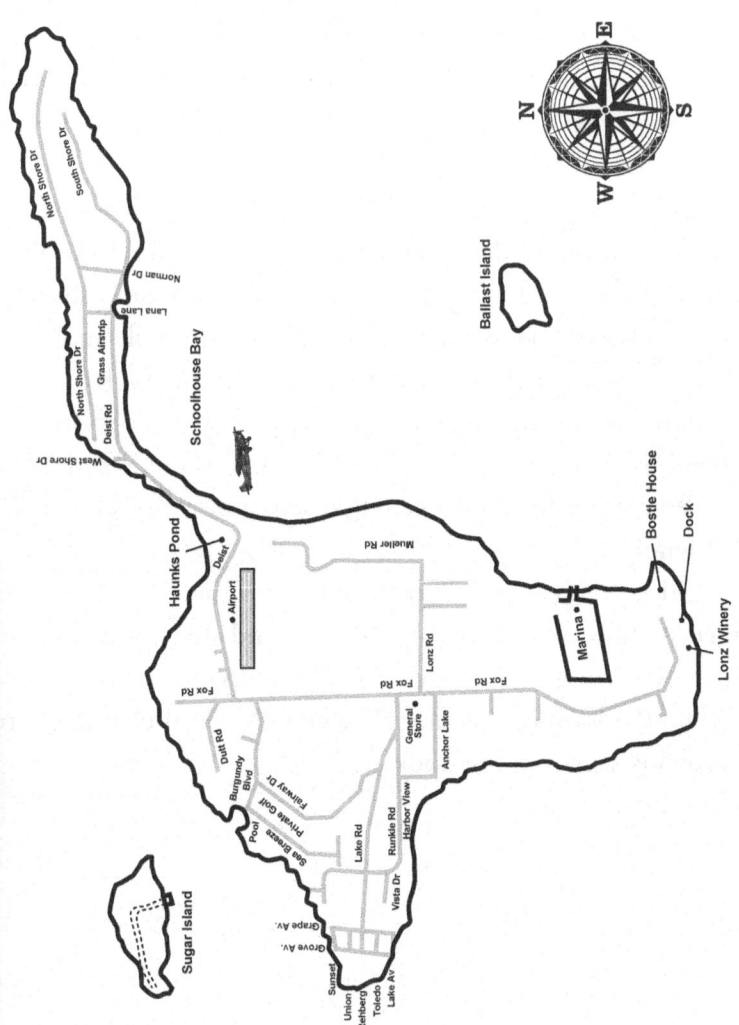

Preface

Over the years, I received numerous comments about Middle Bass Island not being included in scenes in my novels. In 2021, islander Dave Nostrant called me and invited me to speak at the Men's Club breakfast and reminded me that I should look for a way to include Middle Bass Island in my novels. I suggested that I could include Middle Bass Island in this novel and asked for his assistance.

Dave set up an interview session for me with local island residents at the Middle Bass Island General Store. I was stunned by the number of folks who showed up and were so gracious with their comments during the session. You will find many of them mentioned or appearing in scenes in the book.

One of the highlights of the trip was the opportunity to spend the night at the home of Mike Gora, the islands' historian. What an interesting evening discussion with Mike and Jean, his wife!

I'd be remiss in not mentioning another island character I met – Eddie Sheller, who owns the island store! When he pulled up a chair to the table where I was interviewing locals, I could tell by the look on his face that he was a real character. You'll enjoy his scenes in the book.

White Spider Night

CHAPTER 1

Late Morning
South Bass Island, Ohio

After crossing the calm blue waters of Lake Erie, the Miller Ferry pulled into the Lime Kiln Dock on a sultry late August morning. There was no breeze and humidity remained high.

As the crew secured the lines and began to lower the ramp for the vehicles and passengers to disembark, Emerson Moore glanced at his aunt who was seated behind him.

"Still sleeping?" Richard Warren, the driver of the Ford-150 crew cab pickup truck, asked Moore.

Moore, who was on extended personal leave as an investigative reporter for *The Washington Post*, earlier had called his friend from Key West. He arranged for the bearded, island cigar maker to pick up him and his Aunt Anne at Cleveland Hopkins International Airport when they landed the next day. Moore and his aunt were returning to Put-In-Bay after an exhaustive search following her recent house fire and kidnapping. With the help of his closest friends, Moore successfully located and rescued his beloved aunt in Key West during a spectacular firefight and assault upon her captors.

The recent house fire, which coincided with his aunt's kidnapping, caused both to become homeless as he had been living with her near Perry's Monument. His immediate recourse had been to relocate temporarily to Warren's combination residence and cigar museum located across the road from the island airport. She planned on staying with her friends, Ada and Henry Hoover, at their Doorbell Inn bed and breakfast located in town.

"Yes, Richard. She looks so peaceful after what she's been through," Moore commented as he twisted around in his seat.

"She should be glad that she has a nephew like you to come to her rescue," Warren complimented.

Suddenly an explosion and multiple rounds of gunfire could be heard in the near distance. The loud exchange woke Aunt Anne.

"What's going on? What's that noise? Fireworks?" she asked as her slumber ended abruptly.

Moore looked at Warren who shrugged his shoulders. "I don't know Aunt Anne, but you better hunker down," he instructed as she ducked behind the front seat while Warren stepped out of the Ford-150 truck and walked to the side of the ferry for a better view. "You better come with me, Emerson," he called with a sly smile.

Moore joined him and looked in the direction that Warren was pointing.

The building housing Island Bike and Cart Rental, which was located at the top of the hill above the Lime Kiln Dock, was ablaze. Black smoke quickly began to fill the sky as dock workers and waiting ferry passengers screamed and ran for cover. A 6-passenger Club Car golf cart could be seen screaming down the hill toward the Miller Boat Line landing below.

Behind it a short distance in hot pursuit was a racing fuel-powered, high-performance custom golf cart containing three assailants, armed with semi-automatic weapons. Their guns fired continually as they quickly neared the lead golf cart.

"We've got them now!" exclaimed a grim-faced Billy Market, one of the owners of the Miller Boat Line who, in response to the gunfire, had charged out of the doorway of the nearby freight warehouse. He was armed to the teeth as were five of his crew as they took defensive positions.

The lead golf cart raced down the hill as shots from the pursuing golf cart followed it. It catapulted over the edge of the dock as multiple bullets struck and killed the driver. Both driver and the golf cart splashed into the lake and disappeared from sight.

Meanwhile, the high-powered golf cart immediately swung around to drive back up the hill. But the dangerous occupants found their escape route blocked as the other two ferry co-owners, Julene and Scott Market, blocked the top of the hill with their pickup trucks. Scott held an AR-15 in his hands and clenched a lit cigar between his teeth. Julene aimed her hand-held rocket launcher at the golf cart.

Exiting from the cart simultaneously, the three burly men each aimed their weapons at the two groups confronting them. One had a hand-held rocket launcher. As he took careful aim at the pickup trucks blocking their escape route, the Put-in-Bay police department SWAT team's Cobra attack helicopter streaked overhead at low altitude. In response, the man redirected his aim to the helicopter and fired his rocket.

Taking evasive action, the Cobra helicopter sharply pinwheeled in a tight u-turn just above the burning Bike and Cart Rental building. At the same time, Julene fired her hand-held rocket launcher at the high-powered golf cart, causing it to violently explode and killing the three men. SWAT team members then rappelled down to the top of hill where the first of several fire trucks had arrived along Langram Road.

"I think we got it on that take, Julene. Sure scared the hell out of the ferry passengers, didn't we?" director Bob Gatewood guffawed. "Great action. Thanks everyone!" he said as the camera crews wrapped up filming the scenes and the cleaning teams began removing the debris.

"A movie!" Moore exclaimed from where he stood on the ferry.

"Yes. I thought you'd be surprised. They've been filming this scene for the last couple of days."

Overhead, the ferry's sound system crackled. "Thanks for your patience, folks. We thought you'd enjoy a little island excitement before you disembarked. We should be able to get you on your way shortly."

The two men returned to the pickup.

"Is it safe now? Is everything okay? Anyone get hurt?" Aunt Anne peppered the men with questions as she poked her head up from behind the seat.

"They're shooting a movie, Aunt Anne," Moore explained.

"What? And they didn't ask me to play the part of the sultry seductress?" she teased.

The two men chuckled at her remark as the truck drove off the ferry.

"I'm amazed what you went through to find her and save her from those kidnappers," Warren added as he recalled Moore's explanation on the drive from the airport.

"She's a tough cookie."

The forty-year-old, tanned and lean, muscular investigative reporter admitted with a smile. He leaned his head out the open window and let the wind blow through his dark hair.

"You said she's going to stay with Ada while her house is being rebuilt?" Warren asked as he turned right onto Langram Road, heading for his home.

"Yes. We're going to get with Roger Parker and work on

the plans. She has some ideas on what she wants the new place to look like."

"Good. I want you to know, Emerson, that you're welcome to stay at my place as long as you need to."

"Thanks, Richard. I appreciate it, but I don't want to be a bother."

"Bother? You? I scarcely knew you were around when you stayed with me a couple of weeks ago."

Moore glanced into the back seat and saw that his aunt had fallen asleep again.

The pickup truck slowed as it turned into the 300-foot drive that led to Warren's place. A white sign with a caricature of Warren smoking a cigar stood next to the road.

Moore looked to both sides of the drive. "The trailers are gone?"

"Oh yeah. Tom didn't waste any time after they busted that Russian taxi company for selling drugs. He had the DEA in here and they impounded all of those London-style taxis and hauled the two trailers away for additional forensic work."

Warren was referring to the island's chief of police, Tom Ohlemacher, who was a close friend of Moore's.

The truck parked next to the 40x60-foot, nondescript, yellow steel building that housed the island's tobacco museum and served as Warren's home.

"Should we wake her?" Warren asked.

Moore took a quick glance into the back seat. "Let's let her sleep a little longer," he answered as the two men opened the door and stepped out of the truck. Moore grabbed his duffel bag and followed Warren inside.

"You have such a collection of memorabilia here," Moore said as he walked through the open doorway. "Every time I walk in, I see something I hadn't noticed before," Moore commented as looked around the building's interior.

He was greeted on his left by a 1921 Ford Model T roadster, a 1926 Ford Touring sedan and a 1929 Model A Board Huckster with vegetables on display in its wooden bed. He also spied a new addition - a yellow 1939 Packard coupe.

"Hey, isn't that a '39 Packard? Where did you get that?" Moore asked with surprise.

"I'll share that story with you another time, Emerson."

"Doesn't that belong to that island author, Bob?"

"Not anymore," Warren smiled as he walked away and Moore continued to take in the interior. He never tired of it.

The building walls were covered with old cigar signs. The room was filled with antique display cases, containing a variety of cigar boxes dating back to 1888. An antique bar along the back wall held 60 types of bourbon, plus some rum and scotch.

To the right of the doorway was Warren's living quarters. Behind this area was the door to the walk-in humidor. When anyone entered it, the fresh aroma of cigars greeted their nostrils. The climate-controlled room contained more antiques and 8,500 premium, hand-rolled cigars. A separate, but smaller walk-in humidor located elsewhere in the building held another 1,500 cigars.

"I enjoy it," Warren said with a twinkle in his eyes that couldn't be hidden by his eyeglasses. "You know where your room is," Warren smiled. He nodded his head toward the loft where Moore's futon waited.

"I'll be right back. I'm going to freshen up a bit. And Richard, you're quite an amazing individual."

"Thanks," Warren said in his usual low-key style.

As Emerson went to freshen up, Warren pulled up a chair in

the doorway and lit a cigar. While looking outdoors to keep an eye on Aunt Anne, who still was napping inside his truck in the driveway, Warren simply reflected on how blessed his life was. He couldn't imagine the complexity of the task at hand for her to rebuild her beloved home.

Thirty minutes later, Moore reappeared and was freshly shaved and showered. "Is she awake?"

"I think she's awaking. I saw her shift around a couple of times," Warren answered.

Moore then walked outside. "Aunt Anne? Are you awake?" Moore called out softly as he approached the vehicle.

Suddenly, a gray-haired head popped into view. The sixty-six-year-old's wrinkled face had a smile. Her sparkling brown eyes were the hue of comforting memories in the fall. She tipped back her head and roared with laughter.

"What year is this? I do believe I slept into the next year. My, was I ever tired!" she exclaimed as she sat up and opened the truck door.

Moore laughed softly at his aunt as he helped her step out of the truck. He was so proud of her indefatigable approach to life. Nothing kept her down. She had such a positive outlook that helped her overcome any negative incidents. She was a true overcomer.

She was a five-foot-three powerhouse of energy who smiled easily. Her charismatic personality and wisdom drew others to her as they would seek her for advice. She rarely sat still. She loved cooking and baking for others and would be the first to volunteer to help local island groups or lead sing-a-longs.

"You certainly were tired," Moore agreed. "Ready to head over to Ada's?"

"Yes, and let's be quick about it."

Moore escorted his aunt into Warren's home where she was warmly greeted with a gentle smile.

"Please, may I use your bathroom?"

"Of course, you may, Anne. It's the first door down on the right."

"Thank you, dear Richard," she said. "I just hope I don't leave a trail on the way," she teased.

Both men laughed.

"They don't make women like her anymore," Warren chuckled.

"She's one of a kind," Moore agreed.

While they waited for her return, Moore returned outside and transferred her small suitcase from the truck to his red Mustang convertible that was parked nearby at the head of the driveway. Within minutes, she returned and thanked Warren for the ride from the airport. Aunt Anne walked outside where she joined her nephew and entered his car for the ride to Ada's.

When they reached the intersection with Delaware Avenue, Moore turned to his aunt and offered, "Would you like to drive over and see what remains of your home before we go to Ada's?"

"Sure. I'd like to see ground zero and what's left. You said the garage was intact, right?"

"It is," Moore answered as he drove up to the next intersection and turned. right.

As they drove past Perry's Monument, Aunt Anne was craning her neck to where the road ahead took a sharp turn to the right. If you missed the turn, you would have driven through a wire fence and into the side of her house, which was known as Seven Gables.

The house had been built in 1885 by Toledo railroad man

James Monroe. Two U.S. presidents, William Howard Taft and Rutherford B. Hayes, each had been guests at the house.

The two-story home was painted taupe with white trim. It had a massive enclosed porch that overlooked boat traffic entering the bay between East Point and Gibraltar Island.

As they neared the turn, Aunt Anne's eyes brimmed with tears. "There's nothing left," she said sadly as she allowed herself to feel the pain of losing her home.

Moore turned left into the lane and parked in front of the garage. As they left the vehicle, she quickly recovered and forced her mind to switch to positive mode.

"Time to close this old book and open a new book," she said in a firm tone, surveying the burned debris from the house. "I get to develop what this book will look like, though life has no obligation to give us what we expect."

Moore placed his arm around her shoulder. "I know a popular island author who can help you develop that new book," he offered.

She thought a moment. "You mean that bald guy with a big smile? Writes those high-action, mystery adventures?"

"Yes."

"Nice guy. I like him. He can really turn a phrase. We've read some of his books at our O.W.L.S. meetings."

"Old Women's Literary Society?" Moore chuckled.

"Yes, but I'm thinking I need someone who knows home design and carpentry like Roger Parker."

"Roger will do a great job for you. He has a great reputation for building homes on the island."

Aunt Anne continued to forlornly look around her property. In spite of her toughness and generally positive demeanor, she could barely console herself among a flood of memories that rushed through her in recounting what her home had truly meant to her. She persevered and noted, "The fence is gone and so is the Seven Gables sign."

"Not quite. I found the sign and cleaned it up. It's on a shelf in the garage."

She patted his arm. "That's my nephew."

"The trees by the bay aren't damaged nor is the dock," Moore said as he tried to replicate her positive attitude.

She nodded as she took one last look around the property. "I think I'm ready to head over to Ada's."

The two returned to the car and headed back to Delaware Avenue.

CHAPTER 2

Five Minutes Later
The Doorbell Inn

"Have you been to Ada's B&B? It's called the Doorbell Inn."

"I haven't been inside, but I've been to the public beach a few times," Moore answered as he recalled the inn's location near the end of Delaware Avenue. "It's right next to the Spider's Web B&B," Moore added.

"Emerson Moore!" Aunt Anne exclaimed. "Of course, you would know about the Spider's Web! Would it have anything to do with Elke White? Is that the reason for going to that beach? Trying to catch her sunbathing topless?" She fired questions at her red-faced nephew about the German beauty's penchant for tanning European-style.

"No. No, Aunt Anne. I just enjoy that beach. Not too many people frequent it, especially during the week," he responded defensively.

He knew the story about the owners of the Spider's Web B&B. Herman White, who went by the nickname of Spider and was known for having a sour disposition, once was a bartender at the island's Round House Bar. Spider had met the striking forty-five-year-old Elke ten years ago when she first visited the island from Germany. Against the concerns of her close friends, she quickly fell in love with Spider, who then pursued her relentlessly.

She was flattered by the attention and spent a romantic summer on the island with him. It was long-rumored that Spider targeted her when he learned of her inheritance. As the summer season ended on the island, he accompanied her to Germany where they were married and soon sold her family home. She had no living relatives. They spent the winter traveling in Italy and the Greek islands.

When the newlywed couple returned to Put-in-Bay the following spring, Spider had convinced her to buy the B&B at the end of Delaware Avenue. Spider renamed it the Spider's Web and quit his job at the bar. The attractive, long-haired blonde with striking blue eyes that sparkled like diamonds had quickly fit into the island community and became involved with a number of local fundraising events, which soon became a point of contention with Spider.

He didn't like her making monetary donations. He didn't like her flirtatious nature either and was highly jealous of how easily she made friends. Guys were especially attracted to her and Spider was sure it was because of her ample chest. Elke was aware of how men looked at her and enjoyed their attention, but she was also a kind and giving woman. She loved helping others.

As Moore turned onto Delaware, his aunt warned him. "I'll be watching you to see if you come looking for Elke."

"Aunt Anne. You know me better than that. Besides, she's a married woman," Moore mildly protested.

"Hmmm. Seems like I remember a certain married woman named Martine with whom you became enamored during all that mess on Gibraltar Island some time ago."

Moore glanced sideways at his aunt with a small grin. "I forgot," he acknowledged. He then briefly recalled in his thoughts of the instant attraction the two developed for each other when they first met several years earlier.

"How convenient! A tiger can't change its stripes," she suggested as he pulled into and parked in the driveway of the Doorbell Inn.

Before Moore could respond, the front door of the inn opened and a sixty-year-old, brown-haired woman with green eyes stepped onto the large porch.

"Anne! I was sick to death about your disappearance. I'm so glad that you're okay," Ada called out as Aunt Anne walked up the steps to greet her with a hug.

"Thanks to Emerson and his band of merry men, including my honey Mad Dog Adams. They rescued me," Aunt Anne beamed. "And wait until I tell you about 'Big Daddy' Charles Meier from Key West!"

"I can't wait! We have so much catching up to do," Ada exclaimed with glee.

"We do," Aunt Anne agreed.

"Anne, I'm so sorry about the loss of your beautiful home! You must be heartbroken!" Ada said in a caring tone.

Aunt Anne allowed a small smile on her face. "You know Ada, I was just telling Emerson that home is where the heart is. I'm alive and that's what counts, plus no one was injured. You just suck it up and rebuild. When Frank was alive and we lived on the mainland, we lost our house there, too. A tornado went through it. We rebuilt. No matter what happens, life goes on. You just deal with the cards you're dealt."

Moore beamed at his aunt's comments. He was so proud of her resiliency.

"Well, come on inside and let's make you at home."

A noisy, tiny tweet stopped Aunt Anne in her tracks. She turned and with a bit of amusement saw a parakeet perched nearby in a cage.

"Ada, you have a parakeet!" Aunt Anne squealed in delight as she bent over to look at it.

"I do. That's my little Beak-a-doo. She loves being outside," Ada beamed as Aunt Anne admired the bird.

"Hello Beak-a-doo. You are just the cutest thing," Aunt Anne said as she touched the side of the cage.

The bird reacted by pecking her finger, causing Aunt Anne to quickly withdraw it. "Ouch!"

"I should have warned you. She likes to peck people."

"It's nothing," Aunt Anne commented as she checked her finger.

"I have one of our rooms reserved for you for as long as you need it," Ada offered as she hustled Aunt Anne inside.

Moore grabbed her suitcase from his car. As he stepped onto the porch, he paused to take in the view of the lake and public beach. What a great place to watch the sunrise, he thought as he looked toward the horizon and took in the Spider's Web next door. It was located directly on the water's edge.

Moore turned his attention back to the Doorbell Inn, a two-story, dark blue house trimmed in white with a large front porch that held eight white, wicker chairs. The first floor featured a large common area with a dining area to the right. In the rear of the house were the owners' quarters and the kitchen.

Upstairs, the inn offered five bedrooms equipped with a queen-sized bed, side chair, small dresser, TV, reading lamp and small closet as well as private bathrooms.

Moore followed the sound of the voices to the rear of the house where the two women were conversing as they sat around the kitchen table. "I'll take her suitcase upstairs. Which room is hers?"

"Number 2. The door should be open. It has a view of the

lake from the two windows," Ada responded as she turned back to her conversation.

Moore walked to the front of the house and took the stairs to the second level. He quickly found the room, deposited the suitcase and returned to the kitchen.

"Emerson, I don't think you've been in here before, have you?" Ada asked.

"Nope. First time here."

Ada stood from her chair. "You need to come out back and see our courtyard. My Henry has such a green thumb. He has done a beautiful job with the landscaping. Let me show you both," she said as she started for the back door.

"I'd love to see it," Aunt Anne said. She and Moore followed Ada outside and into the backyard.

It was a small backyard, but private with a six-foot tall fence around it. The secluded courtyard was bricked and contained several benches, two tables with large yellow umbrellas, a grill for guests and a fountain whose cascading streams of water offered a calming effect. A one-car garage, which served as Henry's workshop, sat at the right.

There were numerous flowering shrubs and plants around the yard. Two trees on the western side of the yard provided shade from the afternoon sun to the courtyard. It was a horticulturist's dream.

"Beautiful! Absolutely beautiful," Aunt Anne raved as she eyed the landscaping.

"I'll say," Moore added. As he looked up, he could see Perry's Monument towering from the park behind the house. "Great view of the monument, too," he added.

Ada chuckled. "The view from on top of the monument caused a problem for our neighbors," she said as she lowered her voice to a near whisper.

"How's that?" Moore asked, not understanding.

"Folks up there can see into Spider's backyard and that's where Elke likes to sunbathe topless. She's German, you know. Europeans think nothing about doing stuff like that. The park staff made a couple of complaints to Spider and he built that slanted roof over the area where she lays out. It blocks the public view of her, but allows her to sun herself," she chuckled softly.

"That's one way to solve a problem," Aunt Anne cracked.

"It's amazing that the park hasn't tried to buy your property or Spider's. They own everything else on this side of the street," Moore commented.

"Oh, but they have. They've been after Spider and us to sell to them, but neither one of us are interested. Especially at the low price they offered!" Ada explained before her attention was distracted as she noticed a ladder propped against the fence. "Henry Hoover!" Ada called out to her husband.

"Yes?" a voice answered from inside the garage.

"Henry Hoover, you get yourself out here. You have some explaining to do."

A sixty-one-year-old, thin man with a receding hairline emerged from the garage. On top of his graying hair sat a pair of gold-framed eyeglasses. He was known for wearing t-shirts with cartoon characters on the front. He had Sponge Bob on his shirt and, as usual, a toothpick in his mouth.

"Did you call me, dear?" Henry inquired as he shuffled toward them.

"Can you tell me why that stepladder is leaning against the fence?" She pointed at the fence between her inn and the Spider's Web. "Are you spying on Elke sunbathing?"

"Oh no, dear. I must have left it out accidently," he exclaimed weakly.

"Accidently my foot. I better not catch you spying on her, you pervert!" Ada warned.

"Oh no. I didn't know she did that the first time I saw her like that," Hoover countered.

"Nor the second or third or fourth time! Tell the truth and shame the Devil. There have been so many times that I've caught you. I'm warning you," she firmly advised.

"Yes, dear. It won't happen again," he said as he quickly grabbed the ladder and took it inside the garage. Henry could not be heard mumbling to himself, "That's not a hill to die on."

"And put your glasses on your face. You know you can't see well enough without them. You're going to trip on something and get hurt."

"Yes, dear," Hoover called from inside the garage.

Moore smiled to himself at the exchange. His eagle eye noticed that there was a hole drilled in the fence and wondered if Hoover would peer through it at Elke, but he wasn't going to ask. The man was in enough trouble with his wife and he suspected that Henry was not a slave to the truth. Moore also wasn't going to bring up the locals' nickname for Hoover -- Hooters Hoover.

When Hoover returned with his glasses reset on his face, he greeted Aunt Anne. "I heard that you'll be staying with us."

"For a while," she answered. "Have you met my nephew, Emerson?"

"I think we've bumped into each other several times on the island," Hoover said as he adjusted his glasses.

"Right," Moore agreed as he noticed that Hoover had a habit for not looking people in the eye. "Thank you both for permitting my aunt to stay with you."

"That's no problem," Ada said. "We're going to have a fine time. She'll be a part of the family." Ada feigned a serious note as she added, "I do have to warn you Anne. If you hear some screeching noise coming out of our downstairs bathroom, it's Henry singing love songs while he's in the shower."

"Oh my," Aunt Anne replied.

"It usually happens after Elke visits with me. When she's here, he looks for every excuse to be around us. I swear I hear him making soft animal noises as he shuffles around the kitchen. I once caught him leaning over her and smelling her hair. In fact, my Henry is like a retired gelding who has been put out to pasture and has difficulty arising from naps, but he still eats with gusto – especially when Elke is nearby. That man has the hots for my neighbor."

"Dear, you're exaggerating," Hoover interjected quietly as he dangled his toothpick between his lips.

"I don't think so, Henry," Ada countered as she turned to Aunt Anne. "Do you know why I named this inn the Doorbell Inn?"

"No."

"Because Henry can be such a ding-dong at times," Ada chuckled.

"You know that death row is a pretty safe place," Henry exclaimed before turning his head away from his wife.

"That's hilarious," Aunt Anne replied as Moore decided to leave. He felt sorry for Henry although he did deserve some of Ada's stern comments. He bid them goodbye and headed for his car.

Ada focused on Aunt Anne. "Anne, we're going to have a lot of girl time. It will be like having a long-lost sister at home with me."

"It will be a lot of fun, but I want to get moving on rebuilding my home," Aunt Anne replied.

"You'll have plenty of time for that. But you are going to have to come with me every day when I go to the Put-in-Bay airport," Ada said as she placed her hand on Aunt Anne's arm.

"Why in ever would you go to the airport every day?"

Ada's eyes flashed a teasing, seductive look. "I go for my daily pat down from the TSA agent. He's quite a hunk!"

"Oh Ada! You are incorrigible," Aunt Anne laughed.

Ada leaned toward Aunt Anne and whispered, "It's the only thrill I get these days. You know, ride it like you stole it! My Henry is out of shape for too much activity if you know what I mean."

"You don't need to go there, Ada."

Ada was on a roll. "I told him that he needs to get in shape. Then he asked me if I wanted chocolate or vanilla. He thought I said to get a shake."

"I bet he was just teasing you," Aunt Anne countered.

"The other morning, he wriggled around in bed and moaned. I thought he was interested and woke right up. I saw him sitting on the edge of the bed and gave him a seductive moan. He stood up and moaned again. Then he burst my bubble when he said he pulled his back muscle again."

Aunt Anne couldn't help laughing at Ada's predicament.

"The other day, I thought he was walking sexy for me in the kitchen. I should have known better. When I asked him about it, he told me that he pulled a muscle in his leg," Ada said, exasperated. "I swear he's as happy as a dead pig in the sunshine."

"Now I see why you go see that TSA agent every day," Aunt Anne commented.

Ada rolled her eyes seductively.

Meanwhile, Moore parked behind the police station on Catawba Avenue and made his way down the stairs to meet with Ohlemacher.

"I'm so glad that we have your aunt back," Ohlemacher said as the 50-year-old sat back in his chair. The gray-bearded police chief enjoyed working with Moore.

"Not half as glad as I am," Moore replied.

"It's not like people go disappearing around here everyday," Ohlemacher added. "Very, very rare."

The two discussed Moore's recent rescue of his aunt in Key West for a few minutes before Ohlemacher changed the topic. "Are you still interested in working with me on cases that come up from time to time?"

"I'd like that, Tom."

"I can make you a reserve officer so you can have access to privileged information, but you can't write about anything unless you clear it with me. Understood?"

"Definitely."

"Usually reserve officers help with events and crowd control. We might pair them up with a regular officer during the summer months when we have large numbers of visitors to the island. But I'd see your role a bit differently. You'd be assigned to work with me on investigations."

"Do I need to go to a police academy or anything like that?" Moore asked.

"No. There are a few forms for you to fill out and I need to run a background check on you. Anything I should be worried about?"

Moore thought back to the time he lost his memory and the murderous hits he pulled off for the mob, but there was no record of him committing those atrocities. He was free and clear.

"I'm good. Nothing to be concerned about. I do have my concealed carry permit and know my way around weapons," Moore offered as he thought back to his clandestine weapons training in Cedar Key, Florida.

"There's no reason that you'd have to carry a weapon in this role. Nor will you have to wear a uniform. As I said, I'd like to use your investigative expertise in helping me solve any cases that might come up. I don't want the sheriff's department or highway patrol involved if I can keep them out of here."

"I understand," Moore said as he picked up the papers Ohlemacher slid across the desk to him.

"Go ahead and read through them and sign them so I can get everything set up. We have a procedure and ethics handbook that you should read and sign off on, too," Ohlemacher added.

Twenty minutes later, Moore emerged from the police station with his handbook in hand. He headed for his car to return to Warren's place for the night.

CHAPTER 3

**The Next Morning
Spider's Web B&B**

After he rinsed the shaving cream from his face, Spider White stared into the mirror. His craggy, tanned, fifty-seven-year-old face had two deep furrows running across its forehead. His hair was salt and pepper gray. The edges of his eyes bore crow's feet.

He turned his head as he studied his face. In his heart, he knew that at this stage in his life, he was a fixer-upper at best. Yesterday, he had to let his belt out another notch. But that was okay. He had plans.

Not only was he married to one of the most beautiful women on the island, but he also had his mistress. As such, he had the best of both worlds, he thought as he smirked at the image in the mirror.

White threw on a black polo shirt. The shirt had the Spider's Web logo, a white spider below the B&B name, on it. He slipped into a pair of denim shorts and boat shoes before heading from the owners' suite into the kitchen.

The Spider's Web B&B was an 1850s-era farmhouse set on the lakeshore with panoramic views. Two large oak trees stood in front of a wraparound porch that offered the best view of the morning sunrises.

The first floor of the home contained the owners' quarters and office at the rear. It also featured a country kitchen which opened to a large common room that spanned the width of the house and provided a sweeping view of the lake through its window-lined wall. An oversized fireplace served as another focal point that contrasted with the heavy wood-beam ceiling.

All four guest rooms with private baths were located on the second floor with two providing lake views. One guest room had a balcony that offered views of the bay. Each room was furnished with a queen bed, TV, dresser, chair and lamp.

Behind the house, guests could enjoy the private outdoor patio. It shared a six-foot tall privacy fence with the Doorbell Inn that continued along the rear of the property to the shoreline. It had stellar lake views, an outdoor fire pit and a hot tub. There were several chairs and tables with red umbrellas and one inviting hammock. Tucked in the corner was Elke's private awning-covered sunbathing area with two lounge chairs.

The right rear corner had a two-car garage that partially blocked the backyard view of the lake. The garage had been divided to house Spider's small workshop and a rental unit named the Cobweb. It was rented for the summer to a thirty-year-old male, Brock Braxton, who worked at one of the island bars.

Braxton was a hunk and he knew it. Ripped abs, tight biceps, well-sculpted form. Women couldn't resist his magnetic personality or blond surfer-boy good looks. He was five foot, ten inches tall. His face was clean-shaven. Nothing was out of place. He typically wore a pair of white-framed sunglasses with mirrored blue lenses which hid his baby blue, bedroom eyes. He knew how to work his female customers for tips, and occasionally, much more.

A 26-foot dock with two boat lifts extended from the shoreline. The lift on the right was an 8,000-pound aluminum, four-post lift with A-Drive hoists. It held a center-console Robalo R200 powerboat fitted with a Yamaha 150-horsepower outboard engine. It was named *Marlin Monroe* and owned by Henry Hoover, who rented the space.

A similar lift with an aluminum roof held Spider's lake classic, a 1970 26-foot Lyman Sleeper, named *Lyman Life*. The lifts were a short walk across the street to the public bathing beach where guests could relax in a beach chair with towels and picnic lunches provided by Elke.

Spider entered the kitchen where he spotted his wife, Elke, leaning against the kitchen sink as she sipped a cup of coffee.

"Goofing off? Don't you have guests waiting for breakfast?" he growled.

"Honey, I just stopped for a second to take a drink of my coffee before it gets cold," she said softly in her German-accented voice. She didn't want to set him off again after their earlier tiff. She expected that half of the island had heard him screaming at her.

She knew that playing up to him in a kind manner would help delay his violent outbursts, especially in front of guests. Many guests wouldn't return to stay again because of his boiling temper. That was one of the reasons their B&B was in financial trouble.

"Where's Marie? Isn't she supposed to be helping you?" Spider snapped in a perturbed manner.

Marie Donley was one of the locals who helped Elke with housekeeping duties. She also worked next door for the Doorbell Inn. The attractive fifty-two-year-old, who wore her graying hair tied back, had garnered a reputation on the island for her housekeeping skills.

"We ran out of milk and Marie ran next door to borrow a gallon," Elke explained. She held back mentioning that she had asked Spider to pick up an extra gallon the previous day. He simply forgot to go to the store. It was no big deal to Elke.

"She's probably over there gabbing," Spider bellowed. "We should fire her."

"I'm okay with that if you're willing to help me with the housekeeping."

"That's women's work!" he stormed.

Just as he finished, the kitchen door opened and in walked Donley.

"Got the milk," Donley said as she began filling a pitcher.

"Thank you, Marie," Elke said appreciatively.

"It's no trouble."

"Are they at full occupancy next door?" Spider asked. "They don't charge enough. They need to raise their rates." It was difficult for him to hide his jealousy at how much more successful the Hoovers were than him.

"Yes. They always are. And they have Anne staying with them. You know she lost her house when it exploded."

"I know," Spider replied indifferently. "I don't know how they can afford letting her stay with them. Are they charging her?" Spider probed.

"I don't know, Spider. I don't get involved with their rates."

"Are our guests down for breakfast?" he asked Elke as he picked up a slice of bacon and began munching on it.

"Yes," Elke answered. "They are starting out with coffee on the porch and watching the sunrise."

"The sun rose three hours ago," Spider murmured before stuffing two more pieces of bacon in his mouth.

"I'll take the milk and bacon into the dining room," Donley offered as she took the plate of bacon from the counter and carried it with the milk pitcher.

Outside, the two guests were finishing their coffee. They had drawn the short straws and had to stay at the Spider's Web while the rest of their group were next door at the Doorbell Inn.

"One thing I'll say about this place is that it has one of the most beautiful views on the lake," Norm Schultz observed. The medium-built man with a thick head of black hair and mustache had served 32 years as the executive director of the Lake Erie Marine Trades Association (LEMTA), which became one of the most active and successful marine trade organizations in the Great Lakes region. He also had established the Boating Associations of Ohio, which sought to increase recreational boating industry awareness among state and federal policy makers, and served 26 years on the Ohio Waterways Safety Council.

Seated next to him was Ken Alvey, who sported thick gray hair and an equally thick mustache. He previously had served as an administrator and chief of Ohio's watercraft agency before retiring and then succeeding Schultz as LEMTA executive director. Alvey had long been well-known among Lake Erie's boating community.

"I couldn't agree more. One of the most beautiful views," Alvey said as he eyed the approaching Elke. "Good morning, Elke."

"Morgen," she replied. "Breakfast is ready in the dining room, gentlemen."

"We'll be right in," Alvey said as he watched her walk away.

"You know I wasn't talking about her, Kenny," Schultz said with a twinkle in his eye.

"I know what you were talking about and I know what I was talking about. Let's go in and grab some chow." Alvey smiled before adding, "I've never seen anyone with such sparkling blue eyes!"

"I noticed them, too. They're like diamonds."

The two men stood and walked inside. They filled their plates and cereal dishes before returning to the porch to enjoy their breakfast amidst a fresh island breeze. When they finished, they ambled next door to meet with the rest of the team to work on publicity for the upcoming Cleveland Boat Show that would be held in the I-X Center just after the start of the new year.

"It's about time you two sleepyheads got over here," a voice greeted them as they approached the porch of the Doorbell Inn. It belonged to current LEMTA executive director Michelle Burke. The vivacious brunette was seated next to her husband, Joe, and barrel-chested Frank Kern, from Mid-America Boating.

"Sleepyheads? Ken and I were up at five and jogged three miles before breakfast," Schultz retorted.

"More like five miles, Norm," Alvey corrected his cohort.

"Hey, where did you get that head of hair?" a deep voice asked from the open doorway of the Doorbell Inn as the man stepped onto the porch. It was the tall, muscular Erik Kyle from Great Lakes Scuttlebutt magazine and now new owner of Latitudes & Attitudes magazine.

"Drinking Sea Foam?" Paul Klein from Lake Erie Living magazine asked as the lean executive followed Kyle onto the porch.

Schultz ran his hand through his thick crop of hair. "How did you know, Paul? Not only is it good for cleaning marine engines, but a few ounces a day cleans my intakes of any harmful residues and lubricates my upper chambers," Schultz quipped.

Burke's husband laughed and asked, "Did you see that Lyman on the boat lift?"

"That's a beaut," Alvey replied.

"Michelle and I have one just like it," Joe affirmed. "It has a cuddy cabin and a 9'1" beam. Her hull is made of marine plywood and lap-straked. The transom and deck are made of mahogany plywood. She's got a V8 Crusader 250-horsepower engine."

"Sounds nice," Alvey said appreciatively. "Have you talked to Spider about his?"

"I'm not sure I'd suggest that," Schultz said solemnly. His brevity had disappeared at the mention of Spider's name. "That guy has a short fuse." Schultz turned to Alvey. "Did you hear him go off on his wife this morning? It sounded like it was coming from the owners' quarters. Nasty. Real nasty."

Alvey nodded. "Something about wasting money."

"I heard him threaten to kill that pretty wife of his," Schultz added with a concerned look. "Something in the milk ain't clean."

"I'm sorry that you had to hear all of that. I wish we could have all stayed here," Michelle said in a serious tone.

"It's no problem for us. We can put up with it for a couple of days."

"I agree," Alvey added.

The front door opened and Ada stuck her head out.

"We have coffee and Danish set up on the patio if you all would like to head around back for your meeting."

"Sounds great," Michelle replied as the group began to make their way around the inn. Klein found himself walking behind Schultz. He playfully reached down and tousled Schultz's hair.

"Hey," Schultz said as he spun to the side.

"Just seeing if it was real," Klein laughed.

"I may have to start drinking that Sea Foam," Kern, who was walking next to Klein, added with a chuckle. "I could use a little thickening."

As they disappeared into the back, Moore pulled into one of the parking spaces in front of the Doorbell Inn. He left his vehicle and entered the inn.

"Aunt Anne. Aunt Anne," he called as he stopped inside the doorway.

His aunt walked around the corner. "There you are. Are we all set?"

"Yes. I called Roger Parker and he is going to meet us at your old place to talk about designing and building your new house."

"Wonderful. I'm anxious to get moving." Then, she added, "Ada and I are going to Port Clinton later today so I can buy some new clothes since I lost virtually everything in the fire."

Moore looked at his watch. "I think we can have you back here in about two hours and you both can catch the ferry before lunchtime."

The pair walked out of the house and drove to the remains of Seven Gables on East Point. When they arrived, Parker was standing next to a table he had set up near the foundation of the old house. Based on an earlier phone conversation, he had sketched out several drawings for Aunt Anne and Emerson to review.

They spent an hour going over his drawings and her ideas. From time to time, Moore offered his ideas for the new house. When they were done, Moore dropped off Aunt Anne and headed to Pasquale's on Delaware for a late breakfast. Afterward, he returned to Richard Warren's place to help him with yardwork.

CHAPTER 4

The Next Morning
Put-in-Bay Police Department

Moore had been summoned to a meeting with Chief Ohlemacher and brought a few pastries that he bought at the bakery on his way in. Moore walked down the steps to the basement level of the Clock Tower Town Hall building on Catawba Avenue where the police department was located.

As Moore pushed open the lobby door, he was surprised to be greeted by a highly-energized German Shepherd puppy. Moore bent down and rubbed its head as the dog twisted to lick his hands.

"Hi pooch. Are you a new recruit?" he asked with a smile.

"I heard that," Ohlemacher said, opening the inner door.

"Future police dog?"

"I don't know. He's a stray. Roger Parker dropped him off this morning. We're trying to find the owner."

Moore set the box of pastries on the small kitchen counter. "Help yourself."

"Coffee?" Ohlemacher asked as he poured a cupful for himself and grabbed one of the pastries.

"Sure."

After Moore got a cup, he followed the chief to his office where they both took a seat.

"What's up?" Moore asked. "Something about that Russian taxi company?" he asked in a joking manner.

Ohlemacher chuckled. "No. I want you to meet someone."

Before the chief could continue, they heard a high-pitched voice whine from the lobby area.

"Oh, for crying out loud. The puppy peed on my shirt!"

Moore looked confused. He was about to ask Ohlemacher what was going on when the chief held up his hand, with his open palm facing Moore.

"Wait a second."

Both men listened as the sound of the falsetto voice appeared to be approaching. They heard someone say, "I just can't believe what happened! That fricking dog was just waiting to pee on me when I picked it up. Why me?"

Moore swung around to face the open office door. A tall, lanky man, who reminded Moore of a string bean, entered. He wore dark-framed eyeglasses on his balding head. His thin face was highlighted by a large angular nose and a protruding lower lip. He held a pastry in one hand.

"The front of your shirt is wet, Abner," the chief observed.

"Yeah. No thanks to that mongrel out front," Abner said as he absent-mindedly reached up with his right hand and scratched his left armpit. After transferring the pastry to his right hand, he held it out to Moore. "Enchante! You want my pastry? I'm not hungry anymore."

Moore quickly shook his head negatively. "No thanks," he answered as he watched the odd man take another look at the pastry, then inhale it in two bites.

"Abner. Meet Emerson Moore. He's a good friend of mine and has been on the island for several years," Ohlemacher said.

"I'm Abner Cranston. That's my Uncle Tommy," the 34-year-old said as he held out his right hand to Moore who, with the greatest amount of reluctance, shook it. "You can call me A.C.," he said with a wink and a nudge.

"I get it. A.C. like in air conditioner because you're so cool, right?" Moore gently ribbed the newcomer. "And, you speak French, n'est pas?"

Cranston allowed a smile to fill his face. "I never thought of it that way, but that really hits the nail on the hammer."

"Head," Moore corrected him as he thought how full of himself Cranston appeared.

"Of course," Cranston said with a disturbed look at having been corrected. He didn't like people correcting him whenever he misspoke.

"I don't recall seeing you around the island. Are you new?" Moore asked.

"That I am. Uncle Tommy needed a really smart addition to the department, so he recruited me. I gave him a break since he was my uncle and accepted the position. I've been recruited so many times in the past few years," he said as he fawned over himself.

He faced his uncle. "You probably have a big crime you need me to solve. Right, Uncle Tommy? You just haven't told me yet?"

It was apparent the man was egotistical and a talker. Before Ohlemacher could answer, Cranston continued. "Yep. I didn't have to go to Harvard Business School to learn how to be a police officer."

Maybe Romper Room, Moore thought quietly.

"Nope. I went to the school of hard knocks. I'm blue collar," he said as he rolled his shoulders in an awkward motion.

"Well Mr. Blue Collar, why don't you tell Emerson about the commotion you created on your first day on the job." Ohlemacher knew that Moore would get a kick out of it.

Cranston's face crinkled up as a serious look covered it. "I was on patrol, getting the lay of the island, you see. I was patrolling down Delaware Avenue when I spotted a number of violations taking place in front of the Round House Bar. I immediately stepped in and began to arrest everyone who was violating Section 4511.48 of the Ohio Revised Code," he boasted proudly. "I could have busted them for violating 4511.50 too, but I let that one pass."

"Abner, would you explain this section to Emerson?" Ohlemacher asked.

"I can quote it exactly. 'Every pedestrian crossing a roadway at any point other than within a marked crosswalk or within an unmarked crosswalk at an intersection shall yield the right of way to all vehicles, trackless trolleys, or streetcars upon the roadway.' The other one is 'Where a sidewalk is provided and its use is practicable, it shall be unlawful for any pedestrian to walk along and upon an adjacent roadway'," he explained in a self-congratulatory manner.

The chief looked at Moore. "I got several calls on his action and had to hustle over there before we had a riot on our hands."

"Good thing you did, Uncle Tommy, because I had a herd of people under arrest. And there was no way a riot was going to take place. I had them all under control," Cranston bragged.

"That is an understatement. He had twenty violators herded on the Round House Bar front porch."

"What happened?" Moore asked wide-eyed.

"I let them go," Ohlemacher replied.

"Can you believe it? The chief of police did not back up his arresting officer!" Cranston fumed.

"It's called riot control, Abner. We don't enforce that law on the island as I told you at the time," Ohlemacher reiterated seriously. "On crowded weekends, there's only so much room on the sidewalks for people."

Moore had a serious look on his face as he asked, "Tom, am I expected to know all of the laws as a reserve officer?" He didn't want to get that deep into the weeds.

"No. No. You'd be teamed with an experienced officer --"

"Like me," Cranston interjected boastfully.

Ohlemacher shook his head negatively. "You'd be working with me most of the time Emerson, but a few times I might have you observing an officer at work --"

"Put him with me. I can show him the ropes," Cranston urged.

The hangman's rope, Moore thought.

"Abner, I'd suggest you get out of that wet, blue-collared shirt and get back on patrol."

"Okay Uncle Tommy."

"One more thing."

"What?"

"I want you and Emerson to meet at the *Sonny S* tomorrow at noon and take a ride over to your assignment on Middle Bass."

"For that stakeout, Uncle Tommy?" Cranston straightened to his full height as a determined look crossed his face.

"For that –" the chief began before Cranston again interrupted.

"Shhh. We don't want anyone to know what we're doing, Uncle Tommy. Might be overheard, you know," he said as his eyes narrowed with a secretive look.

"Okay. You can tell Emerson when you arrive on the island," Ohlemacher agreed.

Cranston looked down at the front of his shirt. "I'm going to excuse myself. I need to get out of this wet shirt." He looked at Emerson. "See you at noon. Don't be late. The ferry doesn't wait," he advised Moore as he turned and left the office.

Moore cocked his head toward Ohlemacher. "What was that?" he asked, not believing the encounter.

Ohlemacher chuckled. "Emerson, 'It is during our darkest moments that we must focus to see the light,' Aristotle once said. That is my oldest sister's son from Toledo. The boy can't keep a job anywhere. Every six months, he's looking for a new job."

"That doesn't surprise me one bit. I gather that he thinks pretty highly of himself."

"He does," Ohlemacher affirmed. "He operates from the gut and is wrong many times. Shoots from the hip when he conducts an investigation. Cynical. Disorganized. Can't find a stable relationship with anyone, but likes to tell people what to do.

"Little naïve, gets flustered easily, has a high level of confidence in his ability. Grossly inept. Socially awkward — hard for him to make friends. Uses large words, or foreign words that people don't understand to make himself look important and smart."

"He's going to be a handful. Couldn't you tell your sister that you don't have an open position?" Moore pleaded.

"That would not fly. She's the opposite of him. She's like a junkyard dog. I caved in to let him work here for a few months. I'm not sure he's going to last 30 days the way he's going."

"I understand that. He reminds me of Barney Fife from Mayberry. You know Tom, the future belongs to those who --"

"Oh, please Emerson, don't go there. I know he sees beauty in his dreams."

"You can take one look at him and know the tray table is not in the upright and locked position," Moore teased.

Ohlemacher rolled his eyes in agreement as he smiled. "That boy spends more time broadcasting than receiving," he quipped about his talkative nephew.

Grinning, Moore asked, "Where's he living?"

"With me on Mitchell Road."

"Better you than me," Moore chuckled as he imagined what Ohlemacher was going through.

"Thanks. He's the only person I know who is so slow that it takes him two hours to watch Sixty Minutes."

Moore laughed softly.

"He was in a relationship."

"What?" Moore asked in surprise.

"Yeah, but it didn't last long."

"Why?"

"He ran his dog over yesterday."

"I'm sorry to hear that. Maybe he can take that puppy in the lobby."

"He's in mourning. He wants a big funeral for the dog, but that's not going to happen."

"Why do you need me to go with him to Middle Bass?" Moore inquired.

"Primarily to keep an eye on him. I don't want him getting in trouble over there. He's already ruffled some feathers here. I had to move quickly to resolve the messes he stirred up," Ohlemacher sighed. "And that boy has no sense of direction. You make sure he doesn't get lost over there."

Moore chuckled softly. "Sounds like he may not make it to the end of the season," Moore offered.

"I don't know. But humor me and go over there with him."

CHAPTER 5

That Afternoon
Doorbell Inn

"You're going to enjoy this, Anne," Ada said with a smile as the two sat on the front porch.

"Every day at this time? Is that what you said?" Aunt Anne asked.

"Almost every day. A little treat for us older women," she said as she looked with an all-knowing smile toward the sidewalk. "You know, those four little words . . . I've taken a lovaah!" She paused before adding, "At least in my dreams!"

The two women didn't have to wait long before Brock Braxton walked into view from around the Spider's Web B&B as he headed for work.

"Hmmm. If only I was twenty years younger," Ada drooled as she watched the hunk approach. When he neared the front of Ada's porch, she called out, "Going to work, Braxton?"

"Yes ma'am," he responded as his baby blue eyes took in the two ladies. "Just like I do almost every day at this time."

"You have a second, honey?" Ada called.

"Sure."

"Come on up here and meet Anne. She's staying with me while her house is rebuilt. It was the one that burnt down on the other side of the monument."

Braxton took the stairs two at a time as he walked over to greet Aunt Anne. "I'm so sorry, Anne. Will it take long to rebuild?"

"I hope not, but I have Ada here to help me out with temporary housing," Aunt Anne smiled as she allowed herself to closely admire his muscular physique. It was barely hidden by the tight shirt that he was wearing.

"Welcome to the neighborhood. And let me know if there's anything I can do to help out. I'm just next door."

"I most certainly will."

Braxton stepped back down to the sidewalk. "I better go or I'll be late to work."

"Nice meeting you," Aunt Anne called as he walked briskly away. Turning to Ada, she giggled, "What a charmer!"

"Look at him. He's got such a cute little butt," Ada said as she pointed at Braxton. "If he was like chocolate sauce, I'd want him drizzled all over me," she cooed.

"Caught you two!" a voice with a German accent shouted.

The two women on the porch turned and saw Elke approaching from next door.

"Just daydreaming. Nice eye candy if you know what I mean," Ada smiled entrancingly.

"I get my eyeful every day. His magnetism helps me get through the day," Elke murmured as she joined the women on the porch and leaned against the wall.

"Lucky you," Ada commented enviously. "What a good-looking man you have staying at your place!"

"Oh, I know. He's the kind of handsome gent that just gets in my bones. He's handsome from the depth of his eyes to the gentleness of his voice," Elke purred. "He is every woman's dream – manly, handsome, sensitive and romantic," she added wistfully.

"Sounds like somebody has a love interest close at hand," Ada observed as she raised an eyebrow and nodded her head toward Elke.

Aunt Anne noticed and began to wonder what kind of relationship Elke actually had with Braxton. Was that a reason for Spider's anger?

When Elke returned to earth, Ada noticed a look of sadness appear on her face. "Are you okay?" Ada asked.

"I'm fine," she said dejectedly as her emotions changed.

"Something's wrong. I hear it in your voice."

"Nothing really. I can handle it."

"Is it Spider? Did he do something?" As Elke turned her head, Ada saw a bruise on the side of her face. "Did he hit you?"

Elke's hand flew to cover the bruise. "I forgot to put some makeup on. I'll be fine, Ada."

"I'll come over there and give him what for," Ada suggested in a serious tone as she started to get to her feet.

"Sit down, Ada. I can handle it. I probably had it coming."

"No woman has physical abuse coming. You need to go and report it to Tom Ohlemacher at the police station," Ada advised her.

"That's right. We'll go with you for moral support if you like," Aunt Anne offered.

Elke shook her head. "No. I can manage."

"I think you're making a mistake, Elke. I've heard Spider screaming at you and not just once. He sounds like he's lost it quite often."

Elke smiled. "Ada, I can handle it." Suddenly a movement out of the corner of her eye caught her attention. "Here comes Rio. I bet he's looking for work."

"He tried sleeping on our porch and I chased him away. He comes by every once in a while, asking to work for food. He gives me the creeps," Ada said nervously.

"Spider doesn't like him around. I try to help him and give him little jobs to do and food. But I know what you mean about being creepy. I've caught him staring at me when he didn't think I was looking." Elke shuddered for a moment, then continued, "I feel sorry for him. People have tried to help him, but he doesn't want to be helped. I just try to be nice to him."

"You be careful around him. You never know when they might turn on you," Ada cautioned.

The three women turned their attention to the scraggily-looking, fifty-year-old with a white beard on his face. He was dressed in scrubby, torn denim jeans and a torn t-shirt from the Calabash band. Always barefooted, he clucked his tongue as he shuffled his feet while pushing an old, rusted grocery cart with squeaking wheels.

Rio Hawkins had arrived on the island that spring as a homeless wanderer. His version of a bed and breakfast was a DeRivera Park bench and whatever he could scrounge from the dumpsters behind the island restaurants.

When he was confronted by the island police about sleeping in the park, he moved to the public beach at the end of Delaware Avenue. He snuggled beneath the stars with an old ragged coat for a blanket, tied around twice with foraged rope. If it rained, he'd find refuge on the nearby Spider's Web B&B porch or under the covered roof by the Chamber of Commerce office, a block away.

"Hello Rio. How are you doing on this beautiful day?" Elke called. She was the type of woman who'd take care of stray cats, dogs and hurting humans. It was part of a sincere and caring nature that helped define her.

Hawkins glanced up at the porch and took in the occupants

with a single sweep, his expressionless grey eyes settling on nothing. "Afternoon," he mumbled.

"Rio, you come up here and meet our new neighbor. We all call her Aunt Anne and she's staying here with Ada for a while," Elke called.

Aunt Anne cringed and tried her best to hide the willies the drifter gave her. "Hello Rio," she greeted him in a low voice.

Hawkins grunted in response to her salutation.

"Are you collecting twigs and sticks today?" Elke asked, knowing that he had a penchant for doing that.

Hawkins nodded his head.

"Why don't you follow me next door and you can pick up some sticks and twigs that fell from our trees. While you do that, I'll put together a picnic lunch for you. How does that sound?" Elke asked warmly.

"Yeah," Hawkins muttered.

"Let's go," Elke said as she bounded down the steps and headed for her house next door with Hawkins following her. Her mood had changed abruptly at the chance to help someone.

As they walked away, Ada turned to Aunt Anne. "She better be careful around him. Did you notice how he looked her up and down, checking her out?"

"I did. She seemed oblivious. I will say this, she seems like she has a big heart."

"That goes without saying. She'd give you the shirt off her back if you needed it."

"There's one other thing I noticed," Aunt Anne commented.

"What?"

"That Rio has terrible breath. I could smell it up here."

Ada chuckled. "You'll notice a lot more about him as he comes around. Just shoo him away."

Watching the poor homeless man walk away made Aunt Anne reflect on her situation compared to his. She was staying in a cozy room with white lace and the fragrance of lavender. Warm croissants, homemade jams and freshly brewed coffee greeted her each morning.

In contrast, Rio's bed and breakfast was the sandy beach or a park bench with his breakfast scrounged from a dumpster behind the market or one of the restaurants. She felt sorry for the man who was shuffling away.

"Poor man," she commented softly.

"What a dichotomy we have here! Rio Hawkins versus Brock Braxton," Ada said as she broke Aunt Anne's depressing thought.

"Did you hear Elke's comments about Braxton? She sounded like a woman in love," Aunt Anne suggested.

"That's nothing new. I've heard her make dreamy comments about him when she visits. It makes me wonder if they are having an affair. The way Spider treats her, he pushes her right into his arms if you ask me."

"I must say that staying here with you is going to be quite an education," Aunt Anne teased. "Lots of drama around here."

"Did I miss anything? Was Elke over here?" Hoover asked eagerly as he stepped on the front porch. His eyes searched around for his gorgeous neighbor.

"Yes, she was here. You missed your opportunity to flirt with her, Henry," Ada scolded softly.

"Not me. I'm just friendly," he protested, disappointed that he had missed an opportunity to interact with Elke.

"Especially when she's sunbathing topless in her back yard!" Ada countered. "Don't lie like a rug, Henry. I see you climb that ladder that's against the fence several times on a sunny afternoon. I'm not blind you know."

Hoover looked at Aunt Anne. "She doesn't believe me when I tell her I'm bird watching."

"And that's not a robin red-breast, it's a double-breasted mattress thrasher, right Henry?" Ada intimated. "There's a few of them living on this island, and many more arrive during tourist season."

Red-faced, Hoover adjusted his eyeglasses, turned and slinked inside.

The two women settled back and continued their suppositions about Elke and Braxton as well as the mentally challenged Rio Hawkins.

Fifteen minutes later, they heard shouting from the Spider's Web. The front door burst open and Hawkins rushed out as fast as he could shuffle his feet. He had a brown lunch bag in his right hand as he clambered down the steps and started toward the intersection of Delaware Avenue and Toledo Avenue.

The front door swung open violently as Spider bolted through it. His rage flooded the air with profanity directed at the escaping Hawkins. Elke ran onto the porch and tried to sooth her emotionally-charged husband.

Even from where they sat next door, the two women could feel the tension and see the tightness in Spider's face and the robotic movement of his angry eyes. Within moments, Elke succeeded in ushering him inside the house.

"I think someone found Rio in his house," Aunt Anne suggested.

"And I bet there's more to the story and we're going to get an earful," Ada said as she nodded her head to an approaching figure. It was Marie Donley, the housekeeper. She was pushing Rio's abandoned grocery cart and parked it in the Doorbell Inn drive.

"Running for the hills, Marie?" Ada asked as Donley walked over to the porch.

"I feel like I just jumped off the Titanic," she quipped.

"What happened over there?" Ada inquired.

"A purely innocent action was misinterpreted. Elke had just given Rio a bag of food and she asked him if he needed a hug because he was looking down in the dumps. He gave her a little smile and she gave him a big hug.

"Then Spider walks in and goes off. It's like he has a clock ticking in his head that's counting down to the next violent explosion. I worry about Elke's safety around him. I don't know why I work there. Well, I guess I do. I work there for Elke. She is just the kindest lady," Donley explained.

"You sure do have a lot of drama going on at this end of the street," Aunt Anne commented.

"Oh honey, you have no idea," Ada retorted.

"I better go unless you need me for any housekeeping, Ada."

"No. We have it handled for today," Ada replied.

"I'll see you tomorrow," Donley said as she began to amble down the street to her home on Toledo Avenue.

The sound of the nearby boat lift being operated caused the two women to look toward the dock. They saw Spider lowering his Lyman into the water. Once she floated free, he jumped aboard. Her noisy engine rumbled to life as he started her, then pushed the throttle forward. The boat leapt out of the water as he angrily rode away.

"Somebody is mad," Aunt Anne surmised as she looked at the boat's wake.

"I bet I know where he's headed," Ada said all-knowingly.

"Where?"

"To see his sweetie pie on Middle Bass Island," Ada stated smugly.

"What?"

"That's the big rumor. I bet I can call over to the dockmaster and he'll tell me if his boat is there. She will pick him up and take him to her house. She tells people that he's a handyman who helps her out. Pretty handy my foot!"

"Who is this she?" Aunt Anne probed.

"Her name is Riley Bostle. She's a widow. Her husband died about a year ago and left her in debt. She's the opposite of Elke. More like a human blackberry bush, all prickly and thorny. I think that's why Spider likes her. She's more like him."

"Do you know her well?"

"No. We know each other, but she's difficult to get close to."

"Is she as pretty as blue-eyed Elke?"

"Honestly, I don't think so. But she's a big flirt. Likes to show men how she can tie a cherry stem with her tongue."

"What? I don't believe it," Aunt Anne said in disbelief.

"One of the guys over there told me that he saw her do it in front of him. Do you know Dave Nostrant?"

"Yes, and his wife Barbara."

"Dave's the one who told me."

Meanwhile, Spider had finished docking at the Middle Bass Island Yacht Club, which was located in the state park marina on the east side of the island.

"Is this a pleasure visit or working visit, Spider?" Dave Salmi, the dockmaster, asked as he helped secure the boat.

"Working visit. I've got to make some repairs for Riley," Spider explained. He didn't want to talk. He was focused on finding Bostle.

"There's a bunch of guys over here that do repair work. She

could call one of them. It'd save you a trip over here," Salmi suggested, although he had his own suspicions as to the real reason she called Spider.

"I don't mind. Need to help out widows, you know," Spider said. He was in no mood for small talk.

Reading Spider's emotionally-charged disposition, Salmi stated, "That's a good thing, Spider. Good luck on the repair." He turned and walked away.

Spider headed for the parking lot where he spotted a tall, svelte brunette leaning against her truck.

Looking around to be sure no one was within earshot, he greeted Riley Bostle. "Hey Babe."

"Did the ride over settle you down?" Bostle asked. "You sounded pretty mad when you called."

"I'm still steamed," Spider admitted. He wanted to throw his arms around her and hold her tight, but he couldn't do it in public. "Let's go," he said as he walked around the truck and entered it.

As she settled into the driver's seat, Bostle decided to ease Spider's tension since she received an earful during their phone conversation on his ride over to the marina. "I can't wait to get you to my place. I'll take your mind off your problems," she teased seductively as the vehicle slowly traveled down Fox Road.

"Oh Baby!" he groaned in delightful reaction.

"Momma's going to take you home and take care of you," she purred.

He tilted his head and threw her a kiss as he grasped her hand.

"Have you decided anything yet about getting that divorce from Elke?"

"I'm working on it."

"You want to be with me all of the time, don't you?" she asked with a feigned look of hurt.

"I do. I'm working on a plan. We should be able to get away with it and be set financially."

"I'm counting on you, Spider," she said as she drove past the Miller Ferry dock to the two-story house that was perched on the south side, near the old Lonz boathouse. It was the sole house at the end of the lane on the state park property.

After she parked in front of the house, Spider stepped out of the truck and took a quick glance across the water to nearby South Bass Island. He always enjoyed the view. As he turned to focus his attention on her, he glanced over the steep bank to the waterline where abandoned cars from the 1950s previously had been placed as a deterrent to shoreline erosion.

Such a waste, he thought as he passionately threw his arms around Bostle. The two kissed deeply and for several minutes before separating.

"I needed that," Spider said as the two walked hand-in-hand toward the house.

"Things have been so stressful," he confided. "How would you like to be in my shoes?"

"Let's go inside and get you out of those shoes," she retorted as she led him inside.

Spider's face broke into a large smile. He really needed to move up the timeline for his plan. He wanted to be free of Elke.

CHAPTER 6

The Next Morning
The Boardwalk Complex

It was a sunny morning with a light, but sticky breeze across the bay when Moore met Cranston at The Boardwalk to board the *Sonny S* for the 12-minute ride to Middle Bass Island.

"Hi Abner."

"No. It's A.C.," Cranston quickly corrected Moore.

"Sorry. Let me start over. Hi A.C."

"That's more like it," Cranston said as he nodded his head. "Time to board," he said, stepping down onto the *Sonny S* deck.

The inter-island ferry, built in 1948, started its life as a commercial fishing boat. The ferry hull was painted white with black and red highlights and was 50-feet long with a 14-foot beam. Her Detroit diesel motor powered her as she transported freight and passengers between Put-in-Bay and the south shore of Middle Bass Island.

"Need a hand, Emerson?" a dark-haired man with a warm smile asked as Moore stepped aboard. It was Captain Bob Schneider. His father, Sonny, and mother, Carrie, started the ferry service years ago.

"Got it, Bob," Moore replied as he noticed a young man with dark curly hair loading freight. "I see you've got Devan busy."

"It runs in the family," he commented as he looked at his son.

"Looks like a hard worker," Moore stated as the boy ignored their comments and continued loading freight aboard the ferry.

"He can outwork a lot of people," his dad said proudly before walking away.

Moore found a seat next to Cranston. "What do you have there, A.C.?" Moore asked as he noticed a green tackle box on the seat between them. "You going fishing? Where's your fishing pole?"

Cranston looked at Moore with a smug smile. "That, my friend, is my snackle box."

"What's a snackle box?"

"My brainstorm," he answered as he opened it and withdrew a thermos bottle. "This here thermos bottle has hot dogs inside it with hot water. Keeps them hot until I'm ready to eat them."

Moore was surprised by Cranston's ingenuity. "That's clever."

"Yeah. I'm just as smart as them red dots," Cranston cracked.

"Red dots? I don't get it."

"Oh, come on Emerson. You know what I'm talking about. Indians. You've seen those Indians walking around the island with them red dots on their forehead. You know what those red dots are for?"

Moore decided to humor Cranston. "I'll bite. What are they for?"

"Well, all they have to do is push that red dot and it gives their brains extra processing power. That's why they are so smart."

"You don't say."

"Yep. I figured that one out all by myself."

Moore sighed. It was going to be a long day, filled with Cranstonisms. He could tell.

Cranston had one more to share with Moore. "You ever hear of that Chinese philosopher, Unconscious?"

"Confucius, you mean."

Cranston's face frowned at being corrected. He then rebounded, "I know that. I was just seeing if you were listening."

"What about him?"

"He says that a man with one chopstick goes hungry." Cranston reached into his snackle box and withdrew two chopsticks. "I'm always prepared. Emerson, that's what life is about. Always be prepared. That's why I'm so successful," Cranston said pretentiously.

Moore just nodded in response.

Two minutes later, Moore was surprised to see Cranston pull off his shoes and socks. He placed his right leg over his left knee and pulled out a pair of toenail clippers.

Stunned, Moore asked, "A.C., what are you doing?"

"I forgot to trim my nails this morning. Uncle Tommy doesn't like me to do it at the breakfast table."

Observing the surprised look on the faces of the other passengers, Moore commented, "I don't think these folks like it either."

"People need to just mind their own business," Cranston said nonchalantly as he clipped away, sending clippings to the deck. "They complained when I did it on a plane flight, too. Can you believe that the flight attendant made me stop?"

"Just like I am. Put those away and put your shoes back on," Schneider snapped as he appeared in front of Cranston.

Cranston had not noticed that one of the passengers complained to the ferry captain who was now looming over him.

"Come on, Bob. I just have one more foot to do," Cranston's high-pitched voice whined.

"You want to swim the rest of the way to Middle Bass?" Schneider asked.

Cranston saw that they were halfway across and reluctantly put away his clippers. "Oh, all right," he said as he started pulling his socks on.

Inwardly, Moore was not looking forward to a day with Cranston.

A moment later, Cranston turned to Moore to share a life truth. "Emerson, I'm going to let you in on a secret."

Moore sighed. "What's that?"

"You can make people think they're strong if you ask them to hug you tight and you fart," Cranston said solemnly.

Moore looked at Cranston, thinking that he was trying to be funny. But there was no doubt that the man was serious. Moore looked at his watch, wondering how he was going to make it through the day.

The ferry slowly made her way to Middle Bass Island's south shore where she docked next to the Miller Ferry dock. The Miller Ferry transported passengers, vehicles and freight from the Catawba dock on the mainland seven miles to the south along the west side of South Bass Island to Middle Bass Island. The two docks were to the east of the famous and former Lonz Winery, which was now owned by the State of Ohio.

Middle Bass Island was discovered by French explorer Robert La Salle in 1679. The 750-acre island lies 1.5 miles south of the international boundary between the U.S. and Canada. It has fewer than 100 year-round residents and 1,000 seasonal residents. The low, green island was a popular and peaceful site for day-trippers and boaters, who used the state park marina.

As the ferry neared the island, Moore enjoyed seeing the Gothic-style stone castle that island winemaker George Lonz built in 1942. That effort, which stood for nearly 60 years, followed a fire which destroyed the previous structure he constructed in 1933. The Lonz family had a history of making wines dating back to 1884. A recreational boat marina was built in 1962 well before the Lonz Winery was included on the National Register of Historic Places in 1986.

Following the tragic collapse of a crowded outdoor terrace in 2000, the winery was permanently closed and vacated. In the following year, the State of Ohio through the Ohio Department of Natural Resources purchased 124 acres of the island that included the marina and the shell of the remaining winery structure. A renovation of the marina led to its expansion to accommodate 190 boat slips and was substantially completed in 2010. The former winery was renovated and reopened in 2017, allowing visitors to tour the 150+-year-old wine cellars as part of the Middle Bass Island State Park.

When the ferry arrived at the dock, A.C. and Moore disembarked with the rest of the passengers. They proceeded to a nearby parking lot where a police car was parked.

"We always keep a vehicle over here so we don't need to worry about trying to ferry one over during an emergency," Cranston explained as he reached in his pocket for the keys. A concerned look then appeared on his face as he patted his pants pockets.

"Did you forget the keys, A.C.?" Moore asked as he fought to suppress a smile.

"Doggone it. I thought I brought them along with me," Cranston sighed.

"I guess we need to catch a ride back then," Moore suggested.

"Hey A.C. You need these?" dockmaster Jim Roesch called out as he approached. He dangled a set of car keys in his hand.

"Yes," Cranston replied as he looked at Moore. "I forgot. We keep extra keys in the ferry office so that we don't have to worry about arriving here without a set."

"Thanks, Jim," Cranston said as he took the keys. "How did you know I needed them?"

"Tom called when he saw that the keys were still on your desk. Have a good day," Roesch said as he returned to the dock.

The two men climbed into the police car and headed down Fox Road. As they neared the town hall at the intersection with Lonz Road, Cranston noticed a large number of golf carts parked by the building.

"Emerson, we're going to stop and investigate what's going on here," Cranston said as he wheeled the vehicle to the side of the road.

The men exited and walked up the steps to the entrance. As they entered, they were greeted by a blonde woman wearing eyeglasses and a smile, Barbara Nostrant.

"Did you come to join us, Emerson?" she asked.

"I wish. I'm actually working with A.C. today," he answered his friend's wife.

"Very important police business," Cranston piped in, annoyed that he was being overlooked. After all, he was the one in a police uniform.

"Is Dave here?" Moore asked as he looked around for her husband.

"He probably would like to be. Ladies only today."

Moore continued. "What do you have going on, Barbara?"

"It's the Old Women's Literary Society meeting. The

O.W.L.S. are having their meeting on Middle Bass this week and Elke White is our guest speaker. She's going to talk about growing up in Germany. You know there's such a strong German connection with the island vineyards and the Germans who planted them here."

"I bet she will do a great job," Moore commented as he looked into the room. He spotted Elke up front talking to several ladies. He then saw his aunt wave at him as she chatted with local islander Karen Brown. She and Ada had ventured over on the special Miller Ferry trip with many of the ladies and their golf carts.

"Barbara, I'm going to make a public safety announcement before we leave," Cranston said in his best authoritative tone. He planted himself in the middle of the main aisle inside the hall entrance.

"Ladies," he called out. He had meant to use a deep, firm voice, but instead his voice squeaked and cracked. "Ladies. If I could have your attention, please."

The room quieted as everyone turned to look at Cranston.

"I just want to remind you ladies that the speed limit on Middle Bass is 25 miles per hour. I don't want to see any of you speeding when you leave your meeting," he said with a serious look on his face.

As the ladies resumed their conversations, Cranston turned to Moore. "We can go now. My official business is concluded."

When Moore started to follow him, he bumped into a tall brunette with a scowl-filled face. It was Riley Bostle. She brushed by Moore and took a seat in the back row.

Somebody has a chip on their shoulder, Moore thought as the two men left the building and drove to the nearby Middle Bass Island General Store.

"Did you hear my speech, Emerson?" Cranston asked excitedly as they rode away.

"Yes, I did." Moore answered.

"Yessiree. I thought they really liked it. I'm surprised they didn't give me a standing ovulation," Cranston cracked with pompous pride.

Moore nodded as he chuckled inwardly at the misuse of the word.

The one-story building with a covered front porch served as the hub of the island. Half of it was a store with hardware, souvenirs, beer, wine, worms, fishing tackle and groceries. The other half contained a restaurant and bar.

Cranston found an empty space in front and parked. "Emerson, you stay here a minute. I need to go and talk to Eddie. I'll be right back," he said as he stepped out of the vehicle. Leaning back in, he spoke in a hushed tone, "Official police business. I'll tell you when I come out."

Moore grinned. He wondered what Cranston was up to. It should be interesting, especially if the store owner, Eddie Sheller, was involved. The dark-haired and very single Sheller was the heartthrob of the island. Good-looking and a charmer. His friendly, charismatic nature served him well in attracting customers to his store which was the central gathering place for island residents.

Cranston returned, jumping into the driver's seat and starting the car. "I've got to reposition the car."

"Why?"

"Speed trap. Eddie told me to park the car on the north side of the building so I can catch the O.W.L.S. speeding back to catch the Miller Ferry to Put-in-Bay."

Moore chuckled quietly at his direction-challenged partner

as the golf carts would not pass the store on their way to the ferry. Sheller had pulled a fast one.

"Emerson, one of the skills I use for effective police work is to build relationships with people. You should try it."

"That's a great idea," Moore feigned.

"Yes sir. Take for instance this hiding spot. Because I earned Eddie's trust and have a good relationship with him, he told me to park here to catch the speeders," Cranston bragged proudly.

Moore just nodded his head.

Cranston settled back in his seat. Five minutes went by and he started fidgeting.

"Are you okay?" Moore asked.

"This speed trap work is boring. Do you want to sing a song while we wait?"

Moore couldn't believe his ears. The last thing he wanted to hear was that whiny voice screeching out a song. "Not really."

"You pick. Go ahead. I know a lot of songs. Even polka songs. I can sing in Polish."

Moore groaned inwardly. "If I pick a song you don't know, can we forget it?"

Cranston allowed a crafty smile to cross his face. "You think you can pull one over of the maestro here? Huh? Go ahead and try," Cranston pushed eagerly.

"Can you sing a cappella?" Moore countered.

"That's not fair! You can't give me an Italian song to sing!" Cranston argued as his eyes bugged out.

"But you said you were going to sing a Polish polka," Moore cracked back.

"Oh, just forget it," he said exasperated.

Cranston reached between the seat and pulled out his snackle box. "We might as well have lunch," he said as he wiped his right hand under his left armpit before unscrewing the thermos packed with hot dogs. He reached in with his fingers. "Ouch. They are hot. Here take one," he said, holding a hot dog in his right hand for Moore.

"I think I'll pass, A.C. I'm going to head inside and get something. You want anything?"

"No. I'm all set," Cranston replied as he dropped the hot dog in a stale bun. When he tore open a ketchup packet, he accidently squirted ketchup on his pants. With a panicked look on his face, he hurriedly poured some of the hot water out of the thermos onto his pant leg. "Ouch!" he said wide-eyed as he looked how he had compounded his problem.

"You okay?" Moore asked as Cranston quickly used a napkin to wipe away the red stain.

"I think it's coming out. I can't have a red stain on my pants. People will think I'm on my monthly cycle," Cranston joked, surprising Moore.

"I can see if they have some tampons for you," Moore cracked with a smile.

"No. No. I don't need that," Cranston's voice squeaked in frustrated response. "You hurry up in there. I'm going to need your help in writing these tickets." He bit into his hot dog bun as Moore walked inside.

Spotting Sheller skipping into the restaurant part of the operation, Moore called out, "Hey Skippy. You pulled a good one on Cranston."

Island residents teased Sheller about skipping through the establishment and often would call him "Skippy."

Sheller stopped and looked at Moore. "Hey Emerson, I didn't know you were here."

"I'm helping A.C."

Laughing, Sheller asked, "So you know what I did to him?"

"Yes. Too funny. He'll be out there waiting all day. You know he's directionally challenged, right?"

"Yep. That's why I did that to him. Don't educate him about where he should be. Those golf carts aren't getting speeding tickets today," he smiled.

"Okay Mr. 411," Moore stated, knowing that the residents and others contacted him for all kinds of information.

"Not today. I feel more like Mr. 911," he teased.

"And Eddie looks like Mr. 911 today," Bill Lodermeier said from behind the bar.

"Probably most days," Sheller smiled. "What can I get you?"

"One of your famous BLTs to go," Moore smiled. "I shouldn't leave A.C. out there by himself too long."

"On it," Sheller said as he skipped to the kitchen.

"Emerson, what brings you out of the inner city to the suburbs?" Dave Nostrant called.

Moore grinned as he turned to spot the island resident at a nearby table. Nostrant liked to refer to Put-in-Bay as the inner city and Middle Bass Island as the suburbs. He was active in a number of organizations on both islands and once had Moore speak at the town hall to the island men's club.

"Trying to keep Officer Cranston out of trouble." Moore noticed quite a few of the residents that he knew and spent a few minutes exchanging greetings with John Petrone, Mitch Bartels, and Mike and Nancy Paul while he waited for his sandwich.

"We're having potluck dinner here tomorrow night if you want to join us, Emerson," Nostrant offered.

"Thank you, but I have plans," Moore replied. "I bet the

kids will be here to find Spaghetti Eddie," he grinned, knowing the nickname the island children used for Sheller.

Lodermeier walked over to Moore. "This island revolves around Eddie. He gets texts all day and night from folks for help. Things like the 'electricity is out' or 'my garbage didn't get picked up.' But he steps in and helps people resolve their issues. He even checks their house when they're off island or mows the lawn or picks up things for others when he's on the mainland."

As Sheller walked over with his sandwich, Moore mentioned, "Eddie, I just got back from Key West. The lady at the Tree Bar sends her regards."

A huge smile crossed Sheller's face.

"You want to tell me why you're smiling?" Moore asked.

"Yeah. Go ahead and tell us, Skippy. We'd like to know more." Lodermeier turned to Moore. "Eddie comes down to Key West for a visit every winter and stays at my place in the Truman Annex. He always makes a point of stopping in the Tree Bar."

"I'm not talking. Enjoy your sandwich, Emerson," Sheller said as he hurriedly skipped away and Lodermeier followed.

When Moore walked out the door, he bumped into Mike and Jean Gora. The tall, bearded man was the Lake Erie Islands historian, a man Moore admired for his knowledge and island photography. He was also the Steering Committee Chair and webmaster for the Great Lakes Islands Alliance, an organization helping the islands build relationships, exchange information and leverage resources.

Moore had spent several evenings, filled with engaging conversations, with the Goras in their lakefront home.

"You make a wrong turn?" the gravely-voiced Gora asked.

"No. I'm helping officer Cranston stay out of trouble."

"That man needs as much help as he can get."

"You coming to the potluck tomorrow?" Jean asked.

"I can't make it, but I'd love to pay you two a visit and hear more of your tales of island lore," Moore answered.

"Sounds good. Give us a call and we'll get it set up," Gora answered as the two walked inside.

Moore noticed Cranston approaching. He had another large red splotch on the front of his pants and a frown on his face.

"More ketchup?" Moore chuckled.

"It's not funny. I'll be right back," he said as he rushed inside to go to the men's room.

Moore walked over to the patrol car and leaned against it. Within a minute he heard the front-end loader behind the car start up. He turned and saw Sheller at the controls. He was wearing a huge smile as he put his finger to his lip. He edged the loader forward and lifted the rear of the police car off the ground a few inches, then shut down the loader.

"Don't say anything," he called as he went back inside.

Moore laughed at the practical joke Sheller was playing on Cranston. He continued to lean on the front of the car.

A few minutes later, Cranston walked out of the building. He was trying to hide the wet spot on the front of his pants with a towel.

"Get it out?" Moore asked.

"Yes, but the front of my pants is soaking wet," Cranston whined as he walked around the front of the vehicle and sat inside. He was so focused on his situation that he didn't notice the rear tires were off the ground.

"You should take a seat, Emerson. We need to be ready to roll," he said as looked toward the street.

"Sure," Moore said as he entered the vehicle.

Five minutes later, Sheller flew by on an ATV. He was wearing sunglasses and a ball cap pulled down on his head to mask who he was.

"We got one!" Cranston screamed excitedly as he started the car and put it in gear while switching on the siren. He stomped the gas pedal to the floor with wide-eyed anticipation at catching the speedster.

With the engine gunned, the back tires just spun in the air. A look of despair crossed Cranston's face. "Now, what's wrong?"

He shifted the car into first gear and tried again. The rear wheels just spun.

"What in the world?" Cranston asked, perplexed with the situation.

Moore was doing his best to stifle his laughter.

Cranston stepped out of the car and walked around to the rear.

"Emerson. Somebody raised the car off the ground," he said as he saw the front bucket of the loader holding up the car. "Did you see who did it?"

"No," Moore replied as innocently as he could.

"I'll be right back." Cranston walked inside the store and returned within a couple of minutes. "This is a fine mess. Eddie has the keys and he won't be back for an hour," he complained as he sat back in the car.

"I guess we'll have to sit here and wait," Moore smiled. "Look at the bright side. Your pants will be dry by the time he gets here." Moore couldn't stop a smile from appearing on his face.

Cranston threw Moore a frown as he rubbed his right hand under his left armpit. "I've got some hot dogs left. You want one?"

"No. I'll just enjoy my BLT," Moore said before biting into his sandwich. After he finished it, he decided to step out of the vehicle.

"Where you going?" Cranston inquired.

"Stretching my legs." Moore actually wished that he was back on South Bass Island and not stuck with Cranston. It felt like a waste of his time.

From his vantage point at the corner of the store, he could see various golf carts and vehicles leaving the town hall. The meeting must be over, he thought.

He then noticed a familiar golf cart pull into a vacant space and park. It was Ada's cart, and she was driving. Aunt Anne was seated next to her, and Elke was in the back seat. She was holding a container on her lap.

Moore walked over to greet them. "Hello ladies. Your meeting must be over."

"It is. You should have joined us," Aunt Anne said as Elke stepped off the cart.

Moore noticed the container was filled with cookies. "For me, Elke?" Moore teased as he stared at her sparkling blue eyes.

The charismatic blonde flashed a warm smile. "Not these, but I'll bake you some if you want to stop by this evening. These are for Eddie and Bill Lodermeier. They're German spice cookies," she explained as she opened the lid and extracted one. "I guess they won't miss one," she said as she handed it to Moore.

He tried it. "That's delicious. I love the taste. Walnuts, raisins and cinnamon." Moore looked at his aunt. "I probably should stop by tonight and see you."

"Ah huh. The only reason you're coming over is to have an excuse to go next door to sample her cookies." Aunt Anne knew her nephew well.

Before he could respond, Elke suggested as she grinned, "I better take this inside before you devour the rest of them." She entered the store.

"That girl has the biggest heart. She heard that Eddie and Bill got a guy off the island in a plane in the middle of the night when he started having chest pains and wanted to do something to thank them," Ada offered.

"That's very kind of her," Moore commented.

"She's like that all of the time. Doing kind things for people on the islands when she hears of a need."

"You probably didn't notice that she had an envelope in her hand?" Aunt Anne asked.

"No. I didn't," Moore replied.

"She's making a donation to the restoration fund for the island's historical building," Aunt Anne explained.

"Yeah, and she does it when she and Spider are hurting financially. If that man could control his temper, he wouldn't run off so many guests at their B&B," Ada added.

An approaching truck turned abruptly into the parking lot, nearly striking Moore, who jumped to the side.

"You shouldn't be blocking parking spaces," Riley Bostle snapped coldly as she exited the truck and gave Moore an icy glare before rushing into the store.

"Barracuda," Ada commented quietly as the door closed behind Bostle.

"That woman sure does have a mean streak," Aunt Anne observed as Elke returned from the general store. The warm glow had disappeared from her face, replaced with a downtrodden look.

"What's wrong, Elke?" Aunt Anne asked as Elke settled into her seat on the golf cart.

"It's nothing."

"I bet Riley had something to do with that response," Ada suggested.

Before Elke could respond, Bostle quickly walked out of the store. She placed two packs of beer in the truck and climbed in without saying a word to the group. She backed out and headed down Fox Road toward her home.

Elke finally spoke. "That woman has it in for me. She is so rude to me."

Ada and Aunt Anne exchanged glances. They suspected that Bostle considered Elke a rival for Spider's affection, but they weren't going to reveal their thoughts. They didn't want to break Elke's heart. They figured that she would find out in due time, if she had already not suspected her husband was having an affair.

"Ada, look at the time. We're going to miss the ferry," Aunt Anne said as she looked at her watch.

"Not the way I can speed," Ada retorted as she started the golf cart. "We've got to run, Emerson."

"See you tonight," Aunt Anne called as she remembered that he would be stopping by to get some freshly-baked German spice cookies.

As the cart backed out and sped down Fox Road, Moore smiled. That's one speeder who won't be caught today, Moore thought. He turned and walked back to Cranston where they waited for Sheller to return.

"I just don't know how the rear of my car ended up in the air," Cranston moaned ten minutes later as Sheller lowered the front-end loader bucket and the rear tires of the police car to the ground.

"Are you sure that you didn't back up onto the bucket?

Did you feel the rear being lifted in the air?" Sheller asked as he jumped off the loader. He was trying to hold back his sheer laughter at the prank he pulled.

"I just don't recall. Do you Emerson?" Cranston asked as he wrinkled his brow.

"I know nothing," Moore replied with a sly grin.

"Hey A.C.," Sheller called.

"Yes?"

"The meeting at the town hall is over and the ladies caught the ferry back to Put-in-Bay."

"They did? Oh, gosh darn. We missed them. Did I fall asleep while we were sitting in the car, Emerson?" a perplexed Cranston asked.

"I do believe I saw you nod off," Moore replied as he played along with Sheller.

"Well, next time you wake me up. I don't want anyone to think they can get away with breaking the speed limit when I'm on duty," Cranston huffed. "We might as well head back to Put-in-Bay," he added as he returned to the car and started it.

"See you later, Eddie," Moore smiled as he joined Cranston.

Sheller waved as the car pulled out on Fox Road.

As they drove by the town hall, Cranston's eyes bulged out. "Emerson! We were on the wrong side of the town hall to catch speeders," he grimaced as he realized his mistake.

"I guess we know for next time," Moore said as he commiserated with Cranston.

"Your darn tooting!"

"A.C., can you beep the horn for me?"

"Why?"

"There's Chris Zeitler," Moore advised as he spotted his friend working in front of his popular J.F. Walleye's restaurant and bar.

"I can do better than that," Cranston laughed as he switched on the siren, causing Zeitler to jump.

"I owe you for that one," Zeitler called as he saw Moore grinning while the police car drove away.

CHAPTER 7

That Evening
Doorbell Inn

"You make sure you bring a couple of those cookies back for Ada and me," Aunt Anne instructed Moore as he descended the porch stairs.

"Don't eat them all," Ada called. She was anxious for one of the cookies.

"You don't have to worry. I'll be right back," Moore called while walking next door.

"That's what all of the men say when they stop by to see Elke," Ada added with a tone of jealousy.

Moore walked up the steps of the Spider's Web B&B and down the side of the porch which faced the lake. As he neared the side door, he heard a voice call from the backyard.

"I'm out back."

Moore walked down the back stairs and around the house. He spotted Elke at a bistro table that had a plate of cookies on it. She had a half-empty bottle of wine on the table. She took a sip from the glass in her right hand.

"Those German spice cookies look good from here," Moore said as he approached her.

"You're lucky that there's any left. I had unexpected help drop by to help me bake them. Or maybe I should say to help sample them for flavor."

Moore wrinkled his brow in not understanding what she meant.

The back door opened and Rio Hawkins walked out. He was smacking his lips with satisfaction. Raising his fingers to his mouth, he licked them clean.

"Did he make my cookies?" Moore asked, looking at the unkempt man.

"He helped me and licked the batter in the bowl and the beaters. Did you finish the dishes, Rio?"

"Yes, Miss Elke," he answered before making a clucking noise with his tongue.

"Did you eat any of the rest of the cookies I made?"

Hawkins didn't reply right away. His eyes were cast downward. "No. Well I did bump the table and a bunch of them slid off the plate onto the floor. I ate them and swept the floor," he explained weakly.

A likely story, Moore thought.

"You better get going before Spider gets back. You know he doesn't like you hanging around."

"Yes, Miss Elke," he said as he descended the steps and started around the corner just as Spider pulled into the drive.

The car came to a screeching stop as Spider's face turned bright red with anger. "What are you doing here?" Spider shouted angrily as he jumped out of the car.

Hawkins didn't reply. He cowered next to the side of the house as Spider ran over and began to pummel him with blows.

"You stay off my property," he raged as he shoved Hawkins to the ground.

"Easy. Easy," Moore said in a calm tone as he ran over to the two men.

Spider glared at Moore as he stepped back from Hawkins. He didn't like Moore intruding in his business.

"There's no need for that," Moore added as he reached

down and helped Hawkins to his feet. "Rio, are you okay?"

"I'm just fine," Hawkins mumbled.

"Do you want to press charges?" Moore asked as he thought about his responsibility as a law enforcement officer.

"No. No. I'm just going to mind my own business," Hawkins replied softly. "I'll just be on my way." With his head bowed, he slowly headed for the public beach.

"It's a good thing he didn't want to press charges," Spider stormed as the two men walked to the courtyard in back of the house. "Elke, what was he doing over here?" Spider raged.

"He was helping." Elke replied. She wasn't going to tell Spider that Rio had been in the house.

"We don't need any help. Our vacancies are up and I don't have money to throw away on people like him. He's worthless!" Spider roared.

Moore didn't want to be in the middle of a family squabble and decided it would be a good time to leave. "Thank you for the cookies," he said as he picked up the plate.

"And you can't be baking for everyone on the island. That costs extra money for us. You trying to make us go bankrupt?"

Before Moore could take another step, Chief Ohlemacher walked into the backyard. Moore, Spider and Elke were surprised to see this unexpected visitor.

"Hello Emerson," he smiled as he greeted Moore. "What are you doing over here?"

Moore held up the plate of cookies. "Picking up some German spice cookies. Want one?"

"In a minute. Just stay put so you can be a witness," Ohlemacher replied.

"Witness? A witness for what?" Moore asked with a perplexed look on his face. He turned his head to look in the same direction as Ohlemacher.

Ohlemacher and Moore could visibly perceive that Spider's temper was boiling.

"I see something has already got you riled up, Spider. You need to take a few deep breaths and calm down," Ohlemacher said in a soft tone.

Reluctantly, Spider complied and took two deep breaths.

"Elke, could you turn your head to the side?" Ohlemacher asked as he walked over to her.

"Why?"

"I heard that you had a big bruise on your cheek."

Her hand flew to cover her cheek. "It's nothing."

"Please. Let me see it."

"Did you go to the police, Elke?" Spider asked incredulously as his anger instantly spiked. He was seething at the thought that she called the police and might consider filing a complaint against him for slapping her.

"I think it's worse than it looks. You did a pretty good job of using make up to cover it," Ohlemacher said after examining the bruise. "Elke, would you like to tell me how you got that nasty bruise?"

Elke's fear-filled eyes looked directly at Spider. "It's nothing."

Noticing Elke's fearful glance at Spider, Ohlemacher spoke. "Emerson, I'd like you to walk Spider around to the front of the house while I talk to her."

"Sure Tom. Come along Spider," Moore said as he motioned for Spider to follow him.

Spider started to pull away, but reluctantly decided to comply. He walked with Moore to the front of the house, steaming the entire time.

victims of domestic abuse are nearly always women – wives and girlfriends. They very frequently try to protect their abuser despite being a victim of someone who often they love. That's likely the situation between Elke and Spider."

"I'd like to help, but I don't know how," Moore commented with concern.

"Just keep your eyes open." Ohlemacher glanced at the plate of cookies in Moore's hand. "Are you going to let me have one of those cookies?"

"Sure. Sure. Take one," Moore offered as he held out the plate.

"Did you happen to notice that we had someone spying on us in the backyard?" Ohlemacher asked.

"No. Who?"

"Henry Hoover. I saw his head pop over the top of the fence a few times. He was taking it all in."

"I heard that's what he does when Elke sunbathes topless, too," Moore added.

"I heard that rumor, but no one has complained," Ohlemacher noted as he examined the fresh cookie. He settled into the police car and took a bite. "These are good. Hey, I heard you had quite an adventure with A.C. today," he smiled as he changed the subject.

"That's an understatement. Please do not assign me to babysitting duty like that again," Moore pleaded to his friend.

"I just wanted you to have a taste of what I have to deal with every day," Ohlemacher chuckled as he started the car and drove away.

Moore's attention was distracted to the public beach. He spotted Hawkins sitting on a bench while he waved at a passing boater.

After they disappeared, Ohlemacher sat in a chair across from Elke. "It's okay now. You can tell me what happened."

Elke's head was bowed. She was trying to mask her fear. It was a survival mechanism that she used in her marriage. Then, she looked up at the police chief.

"Tom, sometimes we only see clear blue skies when the sun shines. I have a lot of cloudy days in my life."

"And is the darkest cloud, Spider?" he probed.

She was quiet as her mind wrestled with a response. "Some days I don't have the strength to make good choices. Those are the days when I have tears coming out of my soul. I do everything I can to overcome my struggles," she cried.

Ohlemacher scooted his chair next to her and placed an arm around her shoulder to comfort her. After a few minutes, she regained her composure.

"Is the source of your struggles, Spider?" Ohlemacher asked again.

"Yes, but I do not want any charges filed against him. I will work it out," she said firmly.

Ohlemacher stood. "I'm here for whenever you need me. Here's my number. Call me and I'll be right over," he said as she stood and took the card.

She gave Ohlemacher a hug. "Thank you, Tom. I'll handl it."

Ohlemacher walked around the house where he fou Moore and Spider. "You can go now, Spider. But get contro that temper of yours," he warned.

"Yeah. Whatever," Spider grunted as he walked away.

The chief and Moore walked to Ohlemacher's police c

"Did she fess up?" Moore asked.

"Nope. She's protecting him. As you likely know Em

WHITE SPIDER NIGHT

Moore walked across the street and down the short beach path. "Hey Rio," Moore greeted Hawkins.

Hawkins cringed, fearing again he was in trouble.

"Relax. I'm sorry that Spider yelled at you that way earlier."

Perceiving that Moore wasn't a threat, Hawkins relaxed.

"I thought you might like a couple more of these cookies you helped make." Moore held out the plate and Hawkins quickly grabbed three cookies.

Mumbling his thanks, he stuffed one in his mouth. When he opened his mouth, Moore got a whiff of his overpowering bad breath.

"You take care now," Moore said as he turned and walked back to the Doorbell Inn.

"You sure did take your time," Aunt Anne teased as he climbed the steps to the porch.

Moore held out the plate to the two women. "Help yourselves," he grinned.

"What was the ruckus next door?" Ada pried. "We could hear the screaming up here. Was Spider out of control again?" She peppered Moore with questions.

"Just a little misunderstanding."

"So little that Tom Ohlemacher had to be called in?" Ada pushed.

"You should probably ask Henry. He took in the whole deal," Moore replied.

"That's my husband, Mr. Snooper," she cracked.

And you are Mrs. Snooper, Moore thought.

"Really. It wasn't anything that you need to be concerned with," Moore said. He was anxious to get back to Warren's and didn't want to engage in any further discussions on the matter.

"I should be going. Why don't you both take one, and I'll

share the rest with Richard when I get home," Moore suggested as the two ladies complied.

Before leaving, Moore asked one more question. "I'm curious. Did either of you say something about Elke's bruise to Tom Ohlemacher?"

"Not me," Aunt Anne replied with a startled look.

"Me neither," added Ada. "Why do you ask? Is that what that was all about?"

"I was just curious. That's all. You ladies enjoy this evening. Looks like a nice sunset," Moore commented as he headed for his golf cart. He wondered who had reported the bruise to Ohlemacher. In a minute, he was on his way to spend a quiet evening with Richard Warren and recover from the day's drama.

CHAPTER 8

**Two Days Later
Round House Bar**

The island was crowded as visitors flocked to it for the three-day Labor Day weekend, the end of the summer tourist season. It was Sunday afternoon, and Moore parked his golf cart behind the Round House Bar on busy Delaware Avenue. It was Put-in-Bay's oldest tavern, serving customers since 1873. Its modern-day popularity traced back to 1944 when the wooden, circular bar was built. Its unique architectural form also featured a bright red, white and blue exterior and a silver-domed roof.

As was customary during many summer weekends, the bar again was jam-packed with revelers and fans who arrived before the start of Mad Dog Adams' early afternoon show. The red neon "Whiskey" sign was alit and the party was getting into high gear.

As Moore approached the rear entrance, he spotted the legendary island entertainer who had been singing, playing guitar and cracking jokes at the famous island watering hole for over forty years. The muscular singer, also known as Put-in-Bay's original "Ziggy Zaggy Man," was wearing a Cayman Islands ball cap, blue shorts and a bright yellow tank top. He wore an earring in one ear, and his graying hair was pulled back in a ponytail. His eyes twinkled like a kid in a candy store. Mad Dog was conversing with several of his adoring female fans as a warm smile emanated from his bearded face.

"You made it back?" Moore called out to his pal. He recently had left Adams and several of their friends in Key West after they rescued Aunt Anne from her kidnappers.

Adams stepped away from the group. "Emerson! Yes. I got back a couple of days ago. I couldn't miss my Labor Day weekend shows."

"Nice crowd."

"The island is packed," he agreed. "How's your aunt doing? She holding up okay? Did she do anything about rebuilding her house?" Adams shot off questions rapid-fire at Moore.

"She's fine and staying over at the Doorbell Inn. Thanks for asking."

"I'll have to stop by and say hello. What about her house?"

"She's had a couple of meetings with Roger Parker, the architect, and she likes what he has shown her. He hopes to start rebuilding it next week."

"I'm glad to hear that. You're back at Richard Warren's, right?"

"Yes. Great guy to spend time with . . . hey, have you met the new police officer on the island?"

"Not sure. There're so many new ones. Who are you talking about, Emerson?"

"His name is Abner Cranston. Goes by A.C. He's Tom Ohlemacher's nephew and the guy is a real trip."

"How's that?"

Moore briefly relayed his recent adventure on Middle Bass Island with Cranston.

Laughing, Adams asked, "Did you resign as a reserve officer because of him? You have better things to do than babysit."

"No. I should, but Tom might need my help. Here's the latest. I was driving by A Dock yesterday and saw one of the police cars parked in front of it. Its lights were flashing. Then I spotted Cranston. He had a bullhorn out and was telling boaters that they had to evacuate the docks. Not what you want to do when the boats are rafted off three abreast on Labor Day weekend."

"Why he'd do that, Emerson?" Adams queried.

"He spotted a frog near the dock and said it was poisonous. So, he was going to have all of the boats leave the area."

"Was it?"

"Yes, but not to humans. It was a pickerel frog. They can produce a toxic skin irritation, but that's all. With their coloring, they look like a leopard. I had to explain it to him and get everybody calmed down. I think the boaters were ready to run him out of town," Moore explained.

"You heard about the poisonous blue frog they found here?" Adams asked. "Jeff Koehler told me about it when I saw him this morning."

"I did. It was a blue poison dart frog over in the pond on Middle Bass. That was a surprise. You usually don't find them this far north."

"It sounds like you had a hopping good time with your buddy, A.C.," Adams cracked.

"There he is," a man called as he and a woman with dark, spiked hair approached the two men.

"D.K.! How are you doing, man?" Adams asked as he greeted Dennis King, who hosted the award-winning trop rock radio show, Island Time, out of Cleveland. Adams had guested several times on the popular broadcast.

"Good. Hello Emerson," King said as he spotted Moore next to Adams.

Moore nodded. "Good. Especially when I'm hanging with Mad Dog!" Moore teased.

"Let me introduce my friend. Meet the Queen of Trop Rock, Linda Robb. She helps host my show. This is her first trip to Put-in-Bay," King commented.

"How do you like Put-in-Bay, Linda?" Adams asked as he turned to Robb.

"Busy place. There's so much to do here. John and I love it. We've been listening to some great music," she answered, referring to her husband.

"And we're going to take in your show now," King added.

"Are you working on a Phlocking of the Faithful?" Moore asked, knowing that King had helped Pittsburgh native Pat Kaley plan some of the Jimmy Buffet-style music festivals on the island.

"Yes, we are. Scouting out sites for next year, plus getting a little R&R."

"Where's your wife, Dennis?" Adams asked as he looked around.

"She's inside with John getting us a good seat."

Adams glanced at his watch. "I better get up there and start the show." He turned to Moore. "You coming down to the Lime Kiln Dock Monday night for the last boat send-off festivities?"

Moore knew about the fanfare surrounding the last Miller Ferry to leave the island on Labor Day night. It was a long-held island tradition to give her a big send-off with music and fireworks even though it no longer signaled the end of the visitor season, which now extended to the end of October and it's ever-popular Halloween holiday celebration.

"Yes. I wouldn't miss it," Moore commented as Adams began walking away and the two visitors entered the Round House Bar. Moore headed for his golf cart.

CHAPTER 9

Labor Day
Spider's Web B&B

Spider had been fuming for a couple of days as a result of the unexpected visit from Tom Ohlemacher about the bruise on Elke's face. His inner turmoil showed as he snapped at Elke any time she neared him. His contempt swept over her like a tidal wave. He even was short with Bostle when he phoned her from his dock.

Seething, he returned to the house where he confronted his wife. "If you want to stir up trouble with the police, I can give you something to complain about," he said as he raised his hand to strike her. The blow missed her when she ducked.

"That's enough. I'm not putting up with this anymore," she screamed at him. She had reached her breaking point.

"Yeah? What are you going to do about it?" The words flew out of his mouth like sharp daggers. His blood pressure was skyrocketing. He was ready for a physical altercation as he clenched his fists.

Her eyes burned like two red coals as she stared at him, but then she fell back. She saw something different in his eyes. Eyes that once sparkled with passion for her, now sizzled like an inferno. They burned hot with aggression.

Her mind raced with thoughts about what to do. If she was cooking and a pot boiled over, she'd reduce the heat and take the lid off to let the steam dissipate. The only way she thought she could handle this fight-or-flight dilemma was to remove herself from the situation. She opted for the latter and expeditiously ran out of the house.

"Try to run from me!" Spider bellowed as he gave chase.

Elke flew down the stairs with him on her heels. When she started to head for the street, she spotted Braxton nearby opening the door to his apartment. She changed direction and ran to him, calling, "Help me, Brock! Help me!"

At a glance, Braxton could see that she was emotional and scared. He also spotted the look of hatred on Spider's face as he hotly pursued her. Braxton stepped aside and held the door open for her. "Go inside. You'll be safe here."

"No, she won't!" Spider roared as he tried to push Braxton aside.

"Stop!" Braxton said in a firm voice as he grabbed both of Spider's arms and restrained him. "Spider, you're out of control, man. Take a few breaths and calm down."

"I'm not out of control," Spider countered angrily as he tried to push Braxton aside. "She's the cause of all of my problems. Let me go. I have the right to inspect your apartment anytime I want and now is the time."

"I tend to disagree with you because of your current state," Braxton said in a firm voice as he tightened his grip on Spider's arms.

Spider stopped and sized up the young man. Braxton was in pretty good shape and could prove to be more of a match in a fight than what Spider would want.

"If you don't calm down, I'm calling the police," Braxton warned Spider in a tone that meant business.

Spider started to boil up, but was able to control it. As he clenched his tension-filled jaw tightly, he knew he didn't want the police here again. It would ruin the plan he was working on.

Spider relaxed a bit. "Go ahead. Talk to the dimwit. I'm

going back inside," he said as he turned in a huff and retreated to his house.

Inside the house, Marie Donley had been cautiously watching the exchange. She had been tiptoeing around that afternoon as she did her housekeeping chores, not wanting to get hit by any of the shrapnel from the ongoing verbal altercation between husband and wife.

It was time now for her to scoot out. She didn't want to be alone in the house with Spider's temper bubbling. She let herself out the front door and ran next door to tell Ada what she had witnessed.

Braxton watched Spider enter the house, then turned and walked into his small studio apartment.

Elke was sobbing as she sat on the edge of his bed.

"I just can't please him. Everything I do is wrong," she cried. Her entire being felt like it had been fractured into pieces. She felt worthless.

Braxton sat next to her and placed an arm around her shoulders to comfort her.

"The guy is just a jerk. I've seen how he treats you," Braxton said in a soothing voice.

"I hide my pain and try to look normal to people. All I do is wear a mask of normality and cope with my problem. It's not getting any better," she moaned.

"I can see your pain. It's in those deep blue eyes of yours. They used to be crystal clear, now they're cloudy," he commiserated with her as he held her tightly.

"I've tried so hard. I want it to work. I want to bring out the best in him. I want to help him get on his feet. I want to give him every chance I can to do the right thing."

"Have you two talked about going for counseling?" Braxton asked.

"He won't go. He says it's me who needs the counseling."

"Have you thought about divorcing him?"

"I can't."

"Why not?"

"We don't have anything. His anger has run off our guests. We're on the verge of bankruptcy," she whimpered as she confided their financial difficulty to him.

Braxton didn't know what to say. He struggled with coming up with reassuring words. His hand moved to her face and began to gently caress it.

In response she moved closer to him. He smelled good as she burrowed her face into his muscular chest. She relished his empathy. Unconsciously, she started to rub his chest. Her fingers unbuttoned his shirt. She reached inside as her fingers traced small circles on his shaven chest.

She pulled back slightly and looked into his eyes. "Let's get this over with," she suddenly purred through her full lips.

An hour later, Ada commented to Aunt Anne as they sat on the Doorbell Inn porch and saw Elke's Mustang convertible drive by. "Did you see who's driving Elke's car?"

"No, but I saw Elke in the passenger seat."

"Mr. Romeo is at the wheel," Ada revealed.

"Brock Braxton?"

"Yep. I wonder where they're going and why he's driving? She doesn't let anyone drive that car of hers."

"What do you think they are up to?" Aunt Anne asked as she watched the car turn left on Toledo Avenue.

"No good if you ask me," Ada replied with narrowing eyes.

CHAPTER 10

Labor Day Evening
Lime Kiln Dock

A crowd had gathered to continue the yearly tradition of sending off the last Miller Ferry of the summer season from its Lime Kiln Dock on the south side of South Bass Island. It was a symbolic seasonal goodbye to island tourists. Once the ramp closed, the ferry pulled about 100 yards offshore and began circling. The familiar blasts from its horn could be heard over the water and nearby on the island as Billy Market set off a large display of fireworks from the end of the dock. Another gorgeous western basin sunset provided the perfect ceremonial backdrop to the festivities.

A few minutes later, the ferry resumed its southerly course for the mainland. Island entertainer Ray Fogg stepped on the nearby stage to play his song "Waves." Several other entertainers, including Allie Market and Westside Steve, also sang a song. The evening wrapped up with entertainer Bob Gatewood singing his "Friends of the Bay."

Moore was standing on the edge of Langram Road where he could look upon the crowd. Mike Adams was next to him.

"Quite a crowd!" Moore said with admiration as the music that had carried up to them was now fading away into the night.

"Always," Adams agreed.

"Good entertainment, too," Moore commented as he listened to the music.

"And another yearly White Spider night," Adams added.

"I've heard that term from time to time on the island. What is that all about?" Moore asked his friend.

Adams allowed a sly grin to slowly cross his face as he leaned toward Moore. "Rumor has it that it started a long time ago. Back in the day, all of the clear booze left in the bottom of the bottles was saved throughout the year for the Labor Day Monday evening celebration. The gin, vodka and clear rum were all mixed together with a wicked smile into a dangerous concoction. They called it White Spider."

"It does sound dangerous."

"It is. Once the last ferry leaves, folks would make their way over to the Round House for a sip. It's a really dangerous mixture that can result in serious memory loss and uncontrollable behavior if more than a sip is ingested by a person. It really should be served with a warning label," Adams chuckled.

"Sounds like something I should stay away from."

"The next day, people will ask each other whether the white spider bit them last night, referring to the nasty hangover that concoction can give," Adams added.

Moore nodded. "Do they still have a White Spider night?" Moore asked.

"That, my friend, you will have to discover on your own," Adams said secretively.

They were interrupted by the sound of screeching tires and immediately turned to find the source of the noise. Moore then loudly moaned.

"What's wrong?" Adams asked.

"I guess you haven't met him yet," Moore explained as Cranston stepped out of the parked police car.

"Hi Emerson," his voice nearly replicated the sound of the

screeching tires. "I got a report of a party over here," he said as he swung his gaze to the crowd below.

"It's the traditional island send off for the last ferry boat on Labor Day," Moore acknowledged. "There's no need for you to go down there, A.C."

Narrowing his eyes, Cranston stared at the crowd below. "I don't know about that, Emerson. I think they need my expertise in crowd control down there."

"Let me introduce you to an island legend," Moore said as he worked to distract Cranston. "Meet Mad Dog Adams."

Cranston placed his hands on his hips as he swiveled to face Adams. "Mad Dog? I've heard of you."

"Hello A.C.," Adams greeted the officer.

Cranston proceeded to look Adams up and down. He then placed his forefinger in the middle of his forehead and squeezed his eyes together.

"Are you okay?" Moore asked.

"I'm using my third eye. It's full of wisdom and can transcend normal thinking when I activate it. Watch and I'll tell you where Mad Dog entertains people," Cranston explained as he tried to impress them.

Moore looked at Adams who rolled his eyes in disbelief. Moore nodded in agreement.

"See anything yet?" Moore asked.

"Not yet, but I'm getting close."

"How about now?" Adams asked impatiently. He wasn't one to suffer fools gladly.

"Nope. Must be out to lunch," Cranston said as he opened his eyes and dropped his hand from his forehead. "I'll just use my amazing detective skill." Cranston looked over Adams one more time.

"I bet I know where you entertain people," he said in a slow drawl.

Adams was really tiring of Cranston's behavior. "Where?"

"Give me the first letter of the place."

"R."

"Red Moon!" Cranston guessed proudly.

"No. Next door at the Round House," Adams replied, tiring of the exchange.

Before Cranston could comment further, his radio squawked. He turned his attention to the message and then back to the two men.

"Sorry, boys. I've got important police work to do. Jeff Koehler's cat has gone missing. I'll find it before anyone else does." Cranston ran to his vehicle and took off with the siren blaring.

"Is he for real?" Adams asked Moore.

"Piece of work, isn't he?" Moore countered as the two wandered over to join the crowd.

CHAPTER 11

**The Next Day
Police Headquarters**

"Elke didn't come home last night. I don't have any idea where she is," Spider reported to Ohlemacher. "I'm worried that something might have happened to her."

"Why do you say that? What makes you suspect that something may have happened to her? When did you see her last?" the chief probed. He wasn't sure that he was buying Spider's comment that he was worried about her.

"Yesterday afternoon. She argued with me. I don't know what was wrong with her. She just went off on me for no reason," Spider lied.

Ohlemacher didn't believe what he was hearing. It was probably the other way around. "Did you physically abuse her?"

"No," Spider shot back quickly.

"What time did you last see her?"

"5:00."

"Where was she?"

"She ran out of the house."

"Where did she go?"

"I don't know," he lied. "I made myself a drink."

"You didn't see her any time after that?"

"No."

"Have you tried calling her on her cell phone?"

"Yes, but there was no answer . . . and I did notice this morning that her car was missing."

"That's a start. Have you driven around the island to see if you could find it anywhere?"

"No."

Strange. If my wife and her car were missing, I certainly would drive around to see if I could find them, Ohlemacher thought.

"I suggest, Spider, that you take a ride around the island and see if you can spot her or her car. I'll do some checking, too. Why don't you check back with me in an hour and we'll see where we stand?"

"Sure. I'll do that."

Spider left the chief's office to do as he was instructed. He knew that he had plenty of secrets to hide and was careful not to share much information with the police. He also knew that in his dealings with Ohlemacher that he had to appear deeply sincere about the disappearance of his wife.

Ohlemacher called two of his officers into his office and asked them to take a look around the island for Elke and her car. He then called Emerson Moore.

"Hello, Tom."

"Did I wake you?" Ohlemacher asked.

Moore laughed. "Not me. I was up early and already took my morning run."

"I wasn't sure with last night being White Spider night," the chief chuckled.

"I passed on participating. I'm an early-to-bed type of guy. What's up?"

"Remember how I told you that I could possibly use your help on an investigation at some point?"

"Yes."

"I need it now."

"Sure. What can I do, Tom?"

Ohlemacher explained what Spider had told him.

"Hang on a second. I'm actually next door to the Spider's Web B&B. I'm going through some of the house building plans with my aunt. Let me ask her and Ada if they know anything."

"Go ahead."

Moore turned to his aunt. "I've got Tom Ohlemacher on my phone. He said Elke didn't come home last night. Did either of you two see or hear anything that could help us locate her?"

The ladies' eyes widened and a smug smile appeared on their faces.

"Doesn't surprise me," Ada started.

"What do you mean?"

"There was a bunch of shouting and screaming next door yesterday afternoon."

"Sounded like a big fight," Aunt Anne added.

"A while after that we saw her go by in her car. Mr. Romeo was driving her car," Ada volunteered.

"Who?" Moore asked.

"Brock Braxton was driving and she was sitting real pretty-like next to him."

"You didn't see them return, did you?"

"No, but we just mind our own business. Don't we, Anne?" Ada asked.

Aunt Anne nodded her head.

Moore smiled to himself as he knew that Ada was the leading island gossiper. He told the chief what the ladies had reported.

"Emerson, could you take a look over there and see if her car is back? I'm going to call down to the Miller Ferry and see if anyone there saw her car take a ride to the mainland yesterday."

"Will do. I'll call back shortly," Emerson replied before hanging up.

"Look out my window, Emerson. There goes Mr. Pretty Boy himself, walking to work probably," Ada said as she pointed.

Moore spun around and saw Braxton ambling down the sidewalk. At least one of them made it back, he thought.

"Interesting. I'm going to check next door. Maybe she's back now." Moore walked out of the house. When he walked around the Spider's Web B&B, he looked at the drive. Elke's Mustang was still missing and so was Spider's car. Moore guessed that Spider was out looking for his wife.

"Can I help you?"

Moore turned and saw Donley standing on the porch. "Hi Marie. I didn't know you were here."

"Somebody has to clean the rooms. It's a shame. Every place on the island was sold out for Labor Day weekend, but this place. They only had two rooms booked, but that makes it easier on me. Spider's temper runs them off. I honestly don't know why I stay on," she rambled.

"Have you seen Elke?"

"No. I just got here about an hour ago. I guess she's off running errands."

"Spider said she didn't come home last night."

"I wouldn't either if I had to live full-time with that ogre," she retorted. In a more serious tone, she added, "They had a big blowout yesterday afternoon. I bet she's left him. It'd serve him right."

"Do you know what it was about?"

"Not really. I do my best to stay out of their arguments. It's mostly Spider instigating them."

"Did he hit her?"

"Not this time," Donley answered.

"Marie, if you do spot her on the island, could you let Tom or me know? We want to be sure she's okay."

"I'd be happy to, Emerson. She's a good person and I hope he doesn't run her off."

Moore nodded in agreement and walked around to the front of the house. He climbed into his golf cart and headed toward the Round House Bar where Braxton worked. Along the way, he called Ohlemacher.

"Yes, Emerson."

"Tom, neither her car nor Spider's car are in the driveway. I ran into Marie Donley and she had something interesting to say."

"What's that?"

"She confirmed that Spider and Elke had a big fight yesterday."

"Was it physical?" Ohlemacher asked.

"No."

"I did hear from the ticket booth at the Lime Kiln Dock."

"Oh?"

"They saw Elke and Braxton drive aboard the 6:00 p.m. ferry to the mainland. No one saw them return. I wonder if they ran off together?" Ohlemacher suggested.

"I don't think so. I just saw Braxton walking on the sidewalk. Probably to work. I'm on my way to the Round House to see what he can tell me."

"Go ahead and let me know," Ohlemacher said as they ended their call.

Moore found a spot behind the Round House to park. He jumped off the golf cart and walked to the rear entrance where he looked inside. He spotted Braxton behind the bar.

"Hey Brock," he called as he approached the bar.

"Yes?" Braxton asked.

After introducing himself, Moore stated, "I'd like to see if you could help me with a question."

"What's that?" Braxton asked with a quizzical look on his face.

"I heard that you drove Elke White off the island on the ferry last night."

Braxton stopped washing the glass in his hand and peered at Moore. "I did. I was helping her out."

Moore eyed Braxton suspiciously. "No one can find her."

Braxton's facial appearance instantly turned into a stony look. "You mean Spider can't find her? Maybe she doesn't want to be found, especially after the way he treats her," he said coldly.

Moore felt the hairs stand on the back of his neck. There was something amiss and it involved Braxton, Moore's gut was telling him.

"I've got work to do," Braxton said as he walked away from Moore.

Moore exited the Round House and stood by his golf cart as he placed another call to Ohlemacher.

"Yes."

"Tom, Braxton isn't opening up to me and he probably won't. I have a sense that he feels I should mind my own business," Moore explained.

Ohlemacher chuckled. "I have a cure for that. I'll be right over. We'll see how he reacts to the chief of police asking him a few questions."

"Great Tom. I'm parked behind the bar."

"Give me a few minutes. I'll be right over."

"Okay."

Ten minutes later, Ohlemacher and Moore walked back into the bar. When Braxton glanced at the uniformed chief, he saw Ohlemacher motion for him to join them outside the rear entrance. Braxton threw down the towel he had in his hand and joined the two men outside.

"What is it now?" Braxton demanded.

"Listen you young pup," Ohlemacher said as he grabbed Braxton by the scruff of his neck. "You don't talk to me in that tone, you understand me?"

Braxton shook his neck loose of the chief's grip. "I get it." In a more mellow tone, he then asked, "What can I do for you?" He realized that Ohlemacher was not someone to disrespect.

"I'd like to have your cooperation in answering a few questions relating to the disappearance of Elke White," Ohlemacher said in a more formal approach.

"I'd be happy to cooperate, Chief," Braxton replied.

"Tell me what happened yesterday afternoon. Did you witness the altercation between Elke and Spider?"

"I didn't see anything, but I heard it. I think the whole island heard them, the way he was carrying on."

"Did he hit her?" Ohlemacher asked.

"Not that I'm aware of and she didn't say anything about being hit."

"Tell me what happened."

"I was leaving the apartment when she came running over to me. Spider was chasing her and I tried to help her. She was crying and very emotional. I let her in my apartment and tried to comfort her," Braxton explained in a defensive tone.

"Were you having an affair with her?" Moore interrupted

Ohlemacher's line of questioning.

"No. Not that I would have minded. She's a beautiful woman, but I've got enough women younger than her chasing me . . . and they don't have the baggage that she has."

"You mean Spider?" Moore asked.

"Yes."

"She was so emotionally upset that she did make an advance on me, but I shut it down real quick. That may not have been a good thing for me to do at the time."

"Why do you say that, Brock?" Ohlemacher asked.

"Rejection. I rejected her. She just crashed more. Then she said she had to get off the island and asked me to drive her."

"And did you?"

"I did. I was trying to help. I don't think she was in any state to drive herself without causing an accident."

"Where did you take her?" Ohlemacher probed.

"I took her on the other side of Port Clinton to the Overboard Bar."

Ohlemacher looked at Moore as he knew that Moore was friends with the owners of the Overboard Bar. "Go ahead," the chief urged.

"We went in there. I tried to get her to eat something, but she just wanted to drink."

"Then what happened?"

"It was getting late and it was White Spider night. I had to get back to the Round House to help out. So, I left her and hitchhiked over to the Jet Express. It was only a mile away. I caught the Jet Express back to the island. You can ask anybody who was here last night. They know I worked until closing."

"The last time you saw her was at the Overboard Bar?"

"Yes."

"Tom, I can catch the Miller Ferry and go see what they can tell us at the Overboard," Moore suggested.

Ohlemacher nodded affirmatively.

"Can I go now? We're starting to get busy," Braxton asked as he glanced inside and saw the growing crowd.

"Yes, you can. Will you be around the next few days?" Ohlemacher asked.

"Yes. I don't have any plans for leaving the island," he said as he walked away.

"I think he's holding back," Ohlemacher mused.

"Me too," Moore agreed.

"Looks like we are one step closer to finding her," Ohlemacher remarked with relief.

"I bet Cory or Lindsay Marie put her up for the night," Moore said, thinking of the Overboard's two owners.

"I hope so," Ohlemacher said.

"I'll head back to Warren's and get my car, then catch the ferry. I'll give you a call when I find out more."

"You want to take A.C. with you?" Ohlemacher teased.

"I thought you were my friend," Moore joked. "No way," he said as the two walked to their vehicles.

CHAPTER 12

That Afternoon
The Overboard Bar & Grill

Moore wasted no time in catching the Miller Ferry and driving to the Overboard Bar & Grille on the west side of Port Clinton. Pulling into the parking lot off West Lakeshore Drive, Moore parked his Mustang convertible at the side of the gray building with a tropical-colored privacy fence. He smiled as he looked at the huge plastic shark that overlooked the outdoor patio. When he walked in, he always felt that he was entering a bar in Key West.

The interior of the bar was painted in a variety of vibrant tropical greens, blues, oranges, yellows and pinks. The tiki-bar décor was definitely island-style. A "Don't Give Up The Ship" sign hung on one wall. The rope winding around the two pillars at the bar was painted a bright blue. A surfboard hung over the bar and below it was a guitar signed by entertainer and musician Jimmy Buffet. Next to Buffet's guitar hung another that was personally autographed by the equally popular, local island entertainer and musician, Mike "Mad Dog" Adams.

"Hi Emerson," Lindsay Marie greeted Moore as he took a seat at the bar. "I'll get a cheeseburger for you," she smiled. She and co-owner Cory Sipert had become fast friends with Moore, who loved their double cheeseburgers, the best in the area.

"You know my weakness," Moore grinned. "Is Cory around?"

"Out back. I'll get him for you," she said as she placed an

iced tea in front of him.

As Moore sipped his tea, the door to the kitchen burst open and out walked the towering Sipert. "Hey Dude! What's happening?"

"One of your cheeseburgers in a few minutes if all goes as planned," Moore cracked.

"I haven't seen you in a while," Sipert said as he walked over to Moore. "You must have been busy."

"I was on assignment in Key West, Cuba and the Delmarva Peninsula," Moore explained. "I've been looking for an excuse to get over here for a cheeseburger."

"Stop in any time. The door is always open for you, Emerson."

"Cory, I have a more serious reason for visiting you," Moore explained as he transitioned away from friendly chatter.

"More serious than one of my cheeseburgers?" Sipert teased.

Moore pulled out his cell phone and displayed a photo of Elke White that Ohlemacher had texted him. "Did you see this lady in here yesterday, Labor Day? Perhaps anytime last night?"

"Oh, I get it. Did she stand you up and not show up for a date on the island with you?" Sipert cracked.

"No. It's more serious. She's disappeared and I'm helping find her to make sure she is safe."

"Yeah. She was in here. She was with a good-looking dude younger than her. They were boozing it up real good."

"Were they getting along?"

"That's an understatement. She was hanging all over him. I was going to tell them to go get a hotel room the way she couldn't keep her hands or lips off him," Sipert related.

"Do you know what time they left?"

Sipert thought for a moment. "I think it was around midnight. They both walked out. Five minutes later, he walked back in. He seemed upset and had two shots. Then he left."

"Did you see them drive away together?"

"Sorry, but I was focused on my customers. I didn't pay any attention to what was going on outside," Sipert explained. "I'm sorry, but that's all I know."

Lindsay Marie returned and placed a brown paper bag in front of Moore. Inside was the cheeseburger. "Refill on the iced tea?" she asked.

"Sure," Moore replied as he took the cheeseburger out of the bag. His mouth was salivating as he looked at the thick sandwich with two burgers, cheese, lettuce and tomatoes between a thick bun.

"I know that look. You just want to enjoy your cheeseburger," Sipert laughed.

"That, I am going to do," Moore replied.

"I've got to get back to the kitchen. Good seeing you, Emerson," Sipert said as he turned to leave.

"Cory, call me if you think of anything else," Moore shouted to the departing Sipert, who acknowledged the comment with a wave of his hand.

Moore turned his attention to savoring the delicious cheeseburger in his hand. Once he finished, he returned to South Bass Island where he placed a call on his cell phone to Tom Ohlemacher. He updated Ohlemacher on what he had learned from Sipert and the two agreed to meet later behind the Round House Bar to talk to Braxton again.

An hour later, Ohlemacher was joined by Moore as they again walked into the rear of the bar and motioned to Braxton to follow him outside.

"What is it now?" an exasperated Braxton asked as the

three stood in the parking lot.

"Emerson did a little checking on your story. It seems like you left a little out."

With a pained appearance on his face, Braxton's eyes darted toward Moore. "Like what?"

"I found some inconsistencies in your story," Moore stated as he closely watched Braxton's reaction.

Braxton surprised Moore by not reacting. "What do you mean?"

"Like how you resisted Elke's advances. I heard she was all over you last night at the Overboard."

Braxton let out a sigh. "I didn't want to say anything. Yeah. It's true. She had way too much to drink. She was very emotional. She couldn't control herself . . . I guess you could say she attacked me," he explained weakly. "I had to fight her off."

Braxton paused for a moment before adding boastfully, "It seems like I'm always fighting off women."

Moore looked at Ohlemacher who gritted his teeth at the explanation. He wanted to roll his eyes, but held off.

"You want us to believe that you were a victim?" Moore asked.

"Yeah. I was just trying to help her out."

Ohlemacher stepped in. "Tell us what happened when you went outside with her."

"I told her that I didn't want anything to do with her and she jumped in her car and drove away. Then I went back in the bar and had a couple of shots before I hitchhiked over to catch the Jet Express," he elaborated.

"That's it?" Ohlemacher pushed.

"Yes," Braxton answered before adding, "she headed toward Toledo."

Ohlemacher nodded his head. "Anything more?"

"No. Not that I can think of," Braxton replied. "Can I go now?"

"There's another issue," Moore interjected.

"You earlier said that after you left the Overboard alone, that you took the Jet Express back here to the island. But Cory Sipert, one of the owners, said you left with Elke about midnight, but then momentarily returned inside the bar alone and had a couple shots, before again leaving for the night."

"So," Braxton remarked.

"So, the Jet Express does not have any runs from the mainland to Put-in-Bay at that time of night. The last ferry departed Port Clinton at 11:45 p.m. Monday night . . . and you weren't on it, were you Brock?"

"Chief, Mr. Moore . . . Cory Sipert was wrong. I did not leave the Overboard about midnight; it was 11 p.m. and I was on board the last ferry boat of the evening back here to the island. May I go back to work now?"

"Yes, Brock. Thank you," Ohlemacher said.

Braxton returned inside as the two men turned to each other.

"What do we do now?" Moore asked.

"I'm going to contact the police departments in the Toledo area and have them keep an eye out for Elke's car. Maybe she went to spend the night with a girlfriend."

"Or one of the folks who have stayed at the Spider's Web B&B that she was close to," Moore suggested.

"Why don't you follow me over for a little talk with Spider."

"Sure," Moore said as the two headed for their vehicles.

When they arrived at Spider's, Ohlemacher parked in the drive while Moore parked in front of the Doorbell Inn. He left his car and joined the chief at Spider's front door.

Reacting to the knock, Spider appeared. "What is it now? Did you find her body?"

Ohlemacher jumped quickly on the comment. "Why did you say that Spider? It sounds like you think she's dead."

"You guys don't exactly look like the smiling sunshine twins, knocking on my door," he snapped quickly. "You need to look in a mirror. You look like undertakers to me," he added haughtily.

Ohlemacher ignored the comment. "Have you heard anything from her?"

"No. Am I supposed to?" he cracked sarcastically.

He doesn't seem like someone who has his loving wife missing - no real concern at all, Moore thought.

"I would hope so," Ohlemacher noted. "The last we've been able to determine is that she perhaps drove off to Toledo. Does she have any friends there? Maybe she's staying with them?"

Spider's brow furrowed as he thought for a moment. "Not really. Her friends, if she had any, were primarily here. She knew a couple of ladies in Port Clinton, but she wasn't close to them."

"Where do you think she'd go, Spider?" Ohlemacher pushed.

"I haven't the slightest idea," he answered without giving it any thought.

"We're trying to find her car. That should help us find her."

"As flighty as she is right now, who knows what she'd do? Maybe drive over Niagara Falls," Spider surmised in an evil tone.

"You keep your eyes and ears open. Be sure to let me know if you become aware of anything that will help us find her. We want to bring her back here safe and sound," Ohlemacher said.

"I guess I can do that," Spider replied furtively.

Seeing no reason for any additional questions at the time, Ohlemacher turned to Moore. "Let's head out."

As the door closed, the two walked down the steps to the sidewalk.

"What do you think?" Ohlemacher asked the unusually quiet Moore.

"It smells."

"My exact thought. He's not interested in her being found."

"I wonder if he has life insurance on her," Moore conjectured.

"We'll ask the next time we talk to him."

A noise from the adjacent Doorbell Inn driveway attracted their attention. They turned and looked. There was Henry Hoover. He was walking toward them.

"Did you find Elke yet?"

"No Henry. We're still looking for her," Ohlemacher replied.

"She's a nice lady. She deserves better than Spider. I've seen how she suffers from him. He has beat her several times. I've noticed it from my side of the fence."

"Is that where you spy on them, Henry?" Moore asked as he remembered seeing the ladder against the fence and Ohlemacher's comment from the other day.

"I don't call it spying. I call it trying to help a neighbor," Hoover countered. "I'd be the first to call you if I saw things really get out of hand," he reassured the two men.

"You make sure that you do just that, Henry," Ohlemacher underscored as Hoover adjusted his spectacles and walked away.

The two men walked to Moore's car and conversed another minute before leaving.

CHAPTER 13

The Next Afternoon
Ohlemacher's Office

Moore hurried down the hall to the chief's office in response to the call that Elke's Mustang had been found. As he entered, Moore said, "Thanks for having me sit in on this Zoom call, Tom."

"You've been a big help in trying to find Elke. It would be only appropriate for you to hear directly what they have," Ohlemacher said as his fingers flew across the keyboard to connect the call.

"Toledo. They found her car in Toledo, but no Elke, right?"

"Right. Here we go," Ohlemacher confirmed as they connected.

The large screen on the wall displayed Detective Paul Pinnicks in Toledo. "Good afternoon, Tom," Pinnicks began.

"Afternoon, Paul. I've got one of my investigators with me. This is Emerson Moore," the chief introduced as Moore waved at the detective. Cutting to the chase, Ohlemacher asked, "What do you have for us?"

"We pulled over a car matching the description of the one that you had us on a lookout for. The plates matched, too. The driver, an African-American male, was Marcel Payne. He's a local who has a record for murder and violent behavior."

"Was Elke with him?" Ohlemacher probed.

"No one was with him. He said he had the owner's permission to drive the vehicle."

"Elke wouldn't let anyone drive that car and she certainly wouldn't loan it out to someone," Ohlemacher interjected.

"She did let Braxton drive it on Labor Day," Moore whispered softly.

Ohlemacher nodded as Pinnicks continued, "We asked for the owner's name and Payne couldn't remember it."

"Did he say where he got the car?" Moore asked.

"Yes. After about thirty minutes of asking him questions and telling him that we suspected he murdered the owner, he changed his story. He then said he didn't know anything about the owner and never saw the owner. It was a crime of opportunity. He got left behind in Port Clinton by some friends and spotted the Mustang in the parking lot of a bar. He broke in and stole it."

"You believe him?" Ohlemacher asked.

"I do somewhat, but there's more. We popped the trunk and we found a purse. It belongs to Elke White, the lady you're looking for. We found something else."

"What's that?" the chief asked.

"There were a couple of blood stains on the floor of the trunk."

"Were they Elke's?" Moore asked quickly.

"We're running a DNA match against what we can from the contents of her purse. We should know shortly."

"Let me know right away," Ohlemacher instructed Pinnicks.

"Will do."

"Did you ask Payne about the blood?" Ohlemacher asked.

"Yes. He panicked. He said that he didn't have anything to do with any blood in that trunk. He said he didn't touch the trunk. He couldn't because he didn't have the keys. He hotwired the car. All he did was steal a car to get home."

"You believe him?" Ohlemacher asked.

"I'm leaning that way. We also checked for fingerprints on the trunk lid."

"Did you find Payne's?" Moore asked.

"No. But we did find three sets. One set belonged to Elke White and one set to a fellow named Brock Braxton."

"Does Braxton have a criminal record?" Moore inquired.

"He does. A few misdemeanors for assault and sexual battery."

Moore raised his eyebrows as he glanced at Ohlemacher. "There's more to our pretty boy than we thought."

Nodding, Ohlemacher asked Pinnicks, "You mentioned a third set of prints. Who do they belong to?"

"A guy in your neck of the woods. Do you know someone named Eddie Sheller?"

Moore's eyes virtually popped out of his head when he heard the name of his friend.

"Yes. We both know him. He's a good guy. I'd be surprised if he has a record other than a record for the number of women swooning over him," the chief smiled.

"He's really one of the icons on Middle Bass Island," Moore added in support of his friend.

"He's clean from a criminal record standpoint," Pinnicks mentioned.

"We'll get in touch with him and let you know what we learn," Ohlemacher said as he prepared to end the call. "Be sure to let me know about that DNA match," he reminded Pinnicks.

"Will do," Pinnicks replied as they ended the call.

Ohlemacher turned to Moore. "Ready to pay a visit to Braxton and Eddie?"

"I'll say."

An hour later, the two men were on Middle Bass Island and talking to Eddie Sheller behind the general store.

"Why so secretive guys?" a confused Sheller asked the two men.

"Eddie, we have some questions for you," Ohlemacher began.

"Sure. Shoot."

"Where were you Labor Day evening?"

"In Port Clinton. I was at the Overboard Bar & Grill. Why?"

"What time did you leave there?"

"After midnight, I guess. I'm not sure. Why?"

"Be patient. Were there any witnesses to you being there?"

"Oh sure. Cory and Lindsay Marie. Rod Althaus and Harley Dave. They all saw me there. Why?"

"Did you step out of the bar for any reason?"

"Yes. I walked outside to get a breath of fresh air."

"Did anything happen while you were outside?"

"Is that what this is all about? Me helping Elke?" Sheller asked.

Moore raised his eyebrows at the comment.

"Tell us what happened," Ohlemacher continued in a serious tone.

"After a minute or so, I heard a thumping sound in the trunk of a blue Mustang convertible. Someone was crying for help. So, I walked over and tried to open the trunk, but I didn't have any keys. I told the person inside, who it turned out to be Elke, how to find the release inside the trunk. She pulled it and the trunk opened. I helped her out. I could see she was bleeding from a nasty bruise on the side of her head. I then found a rag in her trunk and had her hold it against her head."

"Did she say how she got the bruise?"

"She didn't want to talk about it. It was apparent that she had a lot to drink."

Moore interrupted Ohlemacher's line of questioning. "Did you see her inside drinking?"

"Yes. She was drinking pretty heavy with one of the bartenders from Put-in-Bay. I've seen him around, but I don't know his name."

"Did you see the two of them walk out together?" Ohlemacher asked as he resumed his questioning.

"No. I was in the kitchen with Cory a bit. It was pretty crowded in the bar."

"You gave her a rag. What happened next?" Ohlemacher asked.

"She wanted to be left alone. She had her cell phone and said she was going to call someone to pick her up at the dock. You know there's a path through the woods behind the Overboard that takes you to a dock on the Portage River. It would be easy for someone to run over from Put-in-Bay in their boat and pick her up and take her home," Sheller explained.

"The last you saw of her was her walking down that path?" the chief asked. "And again, this was after midnight, Monday night?"

"Yeah. She was wobbling, but was calling someone on her cell phone. She was pretty serious about not wanting any help from me."

Ohlemacher then looked at Moore. "We'll want to check her cell phone call records for that night and conduct a search along that path."

"You think we'll find her on that path?" Moore asked.

"Maybe. It's worth a trip over on the police boat to check,"

Ohlemacher replied as he turned back to Sheller. "Eddie, is there anything else that you can recall about that night that might help us find Elke?"

Sheller cocked his head to the side as he thought. "No, I can't think of anything. You want me to call Cory and ask him to check out the path?" he volunteered.

"No. Please don't. I don't need anyone disturbing any evidence that could be there," the chief advised.

"I'll do anything I can to help you. Elke is a nice lady. Everyone loves her," Sheller confided.

"We know. Keep all of this confidential so nothing mucks up our investigation, okay?" the chief asked.

"You got it," Sheller responded seriously.

The men ended the conversation. As Sheller returned inside the store, Ohlemacher and Moore departed to catch the *Sonny S* ferry back to Put-in-Bay.

While they were on the ferry, Ohlemacher called his office and spoke with his dispatcher. "Karen, I need you to get the cell phone records for Elke White. I'd like to see her calls from Labor Day to the day after, yesterday."

"Okay. I'll get right on it. You had a call from a Detective Paul Pinnicks. He said there was a positive on the DNA match for Elke White. He's emailing you the results."

"Good. Thank you, Karen," the chief said as he ended the call.

"Do you have to get a search warrant to access Elke's phone records?" Moore asked.

"We don't need one for this type of incident. There are traditional search warrant exceptions that apply," Ohlemacher explained.

"I see."

"We did hear back on the DNA identification from Pinnicks. It was a match as I would expect after hearing what Eddie had to say," Ohlemacher added.

"You think Braxton hit her? Maybe was going to kill her? That's why he put her in the trunk?"

"I don't know, but we're going to find out shortly. Next stop will be another visit with Braxton. He's been holding back from us the entire time," Ohlemacher said as the *Sonny S* soon arrived at The Boardwalk.

The men walked around the building to where Ohlemacher's police car was parked. In a few minutes, they drove to the Round House Bar and parked behind it. Ohlemacher summoned Braxton who was working, and asked him again to step outside where he began a new line of questioning.

"Why haven't you told us everything?"

"What do you mean?" Braxton asked uneasily.

"You want to tell me about putting Elke White in the trunk of her car at the Overboard?"

"I don't know anything about that," he said as he looked away with an increased level of nervousness.

"It's not a good thing to lie to a police officer, Brock. I know you put her in the trunk. Tell me want happened," Ohlemacher drilled in.

Braxton looked around the parking lot as he weighed his response. Moore was standing nearby in silence and listening to the exchange.

Sighing, Braxton responded, "It was an accident, sir. We went outside and she fell. She hit her head on the concrete steps and lost consciousness. I didn't know what to do. Here I am with this married woman. Who's going to believe me? I thought she was still breathing and I needed time to think."

"What did you do?"

"I went back inside and had two shots of whiskey. I was only gone about ten minutes. When I came back out, the car was gone. I figured she regained consciousness, then drove to the ferry dock. Actually, I was relieved to think she was okay."

"How did she drive away?" Ohlemacher pushed.

"She started her car and left is my guess."

"Then you left the keys in the car so she could leave?" Ohlemacher probed.

Braxton was quiet for a moment. "No. I had them with me," Braxton responded sheepishly.

"How do you think she drove away then? Did she know how to hotwire a car?"

"I don't know. I wasn't thinking clearly, sir."

"Where are the keys?"

"I tossed them in the Portage River after I boarded the Jet Express," he explained meekly.

"So, the lady that you cared about, you didn't care enough to take better care of her?" a disgusted Ohlemacher exclaimed.

"Listen guys. I made a foolish mistake."

"Stupid mistake if you ask me," Moore interjected. He was repulsed by what he had been hearing.

"I'll be back in touch, Brock. But I'm warning you, you better keep a low profile," Ohlemacher said as he beckoned Moore to follow him. Braxton returned to work in the Round House.

Ohlemacher and Moore went to the car and drove to the Miller Marina to board the police boat. It was a deep-vee, 29-foot Defiant with twin outboard engines that could take the boat to a speed of 50 knots.

Forty minutes later, they were passing under the Port Clinton drawbridge as they headed up the Portage River. As they neared the dock behind the Overboard Bar & Grill, Moore stepped out of the pilothouse. He walked up to the bow and grabbed a mooring line which he threw to one of two Port Clinton police officers standing nearby. Ohlemacher contacted them on the way from Put-in-Bay since the Overboard was in their jurisdiction.

As Moore and an officer secured the lines, Ohlemacher joined them on the dock. "Thanks for meeting us," he said.

"No problem, Tom. We're glad to help," Eric Adams responded. "You have a picture of this missing lady?"

Ohlemacher showed the officers Elke's picture on his cell phone.

"I don't know her. Do you, Ed?" Adams asked as he turned and showed the second officer, Ed Sarley.

"I don't recognize her."

Adams returned the phone to Ohlemacher. "You believe that somebody picked her up here and took her somewhere?" Adams asked as he recalled their recent conversation.

"That's the problem, Eric. All we know is that she is missing. I don't know yet if we are investigating a homicide. We're slowly putting together the pieces to what we believe happened Monday night."

The four men carefully made their way along the path down to the dock. Each was carefully searching for any visible clues. Suddenly, Sarley stopped and pointed.

"There's a cell phone over here." He pointed to the edge of the path where it met the dock. "Looks like it may have been dropped," Sarley confirmed.

Ohlemacher walked over and carefully picked it up with a gloved hand and placed it into an evidence bag. "We'll take this back and see what we can find on it. Maybe it belongs to Elke or maybe it doesn't."

The men continued to search the area and didn't find anything when they reached the parking lot. Moore then excused himself and walked inside the rear of the Overboard.

"Hey Cory," he greeted the owner who was seated at his desk.

"Coming in through the back now, are you?" the smiling owner teased Moore.

"We've been checking out the path, the dock and surrounding area trying to find clues about Elke."

"She hasn't shown up yet?"

"Not yet, Cory. When we talked last, you didn't mention that Eddie Sheller was here late Monday night when she apparently disappeared."

"I didn't think about it. Is that a problem?" Cory asked as he wrinkled his brow.

"The Toledo police found her car and Eddie's fingerprints were on the trunk of the car. Did he say anything to you about her?"

"No, but he doesn't talk a lot about drama. He just gets things done. You think he's involved with her disappearance?"

"I don't know. We talked with him and his explanation seemed plausible," Moore replied. "Did he have his boat tied up at the dock out back?"

"I don't think so. I thought he came over on the ferry with his truck because he was going to pick up supplies for his store yesterday. I'm not sure."

"I didn't think to ask him. I'll follow up. Did you notice any interaction between Eddie, Elke and the guy she was with?"

"Not that I can recall. We were pretty busy . . . You're really getting into this police investigation stuff, aren't you?" Cory inquired.

"More than I would like to. I'm just helping out Tom, plus I know Elke. I just would like to see her found safe and secure."

"Have time for another cheeseburger?" Cory knew how much Moore enjoyed them.

"No. I better go. Tom Ohlemacher is out back, waiting for me," Moore said as he turned to go. "Thanks Cory."

"Any time."

When Moore returned to the dock, he saw Ohlemacher was on his cell phone. The other two officers were returning from a quick search of the shoreline.

"Find anything?" Moore asked as Ohlemacher ended his call.

"Not a thing," Adams replied. "Tom, we're going to do a slow cruise along the shoreline to see if we see anything."

"Thank you. I appreciate it. We've got to return to Put-in-Bay. I'll be in touch," Ohlemacher said as Moore worked quickly to free the lines and jump aboard.

As they eased the craft down the river, Ohlemacher asked, "Did you learn anything interesting from Cory?"

"No. We don't know for sure whether Eddie Sheller came over here that night on his boat or rode over on the ferry before driving here. I wonder if he took Elke home or wherever and isn't telling us."

"That's an interesting reveal."

"We need to see if Eddie is holding back on us. Maybe he has her hidden away so she can think things through," Moore suggested.

"I hope so although I'll be disappointed if we're wasting valuable time when he's taken care of her and didn't tell us," Ohlemacher responded somberly.

"How about you? Anything new?" Moore asked.

"As a matter of fact, there is. Karen just called me. She reviewed the cell phone records and found two calls were made from Elke's phone that night. They were the last calls made from it, too."

"Do you know who the calls were to?"

"Yes. One was to her home phone."

"To Spider?" Moore asked.

"Yes. She probably called to have him pick her up."

"Maybe she calmed down then. Was it a long conversation?"

"Short one. She may have left a message for him to call her."

"What about the other call?"

"This will surprise you, Emerson. She called her neighbor."

"Ada?"

"No, Henry."

"What?"

The chief nodded his head as he guided the police boat out of the mouth of the Portage River into Lake Erie. "It was a short call, too."

"Another voicemail message?"

"Possibly."

Moore shook his head from side to side as Ohlemacher continued. "Emerson, let me give you a what-if."

"Okay." As an investigative reporter and Tom's special assistant, Moore was open to any possible theory or explanation. "What's your theory, Tom?"

"What if she can't get someone to come over and pick her up on the dock? It's late at night. She likely is intoxicated. Maybe she has sustained some sort of head injury? Perhaps drugs may be involved in some fashion. Maybe she was held against her will, briefly."

"Then she has Eddie take her somewhere in his boat," Moore suggested.

"Let's forget about that until we've talked to him again. But what if she gets frustrated, what does she do? She's apparently mad at Braxton so she wouldn't go back inside the bar. Does she start walking to the Jet Express?"

"But Braxton said he walked to the Jet Express."

"Right. Did he see her on the way? Did they have more conflict? I'm sure she'd be upset that he stuffed her in her own trunk."

"Right," Moore agreed.

"Did he dump her somewhere between the Overboard and the Jet Express? We need to talk to the Jet Express people and review video from Monday night. It would be interesting to see if Braxton boarded the Jet Express, when he did and if he was alone."

"Or did she hitchhike somewhere?" Moore proposed. "Maybe got a ride from someone else at the Overboard? Perhaps she was abducted in some manner?"

"I was coming to that," Ohlemacher continued. "You then have all of these condominiums along the road from the bar to the Jet Express. Did she seek refuge in one of them? Is she still hiding in one of them?"

"Maybe it's time that we issue something in the media to seek help in finding her," Moore suggested. "We could use social media, too."

"You read my mind, Emerson. And I think we're going to have to get our friends at the Port Clinton Police Department more involved since she was last seen here."

"I think so."

"But first, we're going back to talk to Spider, Henry and Eddie," Ohlemacher said as the police boat flew across the lake toward South Bass Island.

CHAPTER 14

Early Evening
Spider's Web B&B

Moore and Ohlemacher were standing in Spider's office at the rear of the B&B. Spider had depressed the play key on a phone answering machine and they listened to Elke's slurred message.

"Spider, I need a ride home right away. Can you just forget about our argument and come pick me up in your boat? I'm on the Overboard Bar's dock on the Portage River in Port Clinton."

"Did you pick her up?" Ohlemacher asked.

"No. I had too much to drink and I was passed out in my bed," Spider explained haughtily. "As a matter of fact, I don't check this phone for messages, she does. Why didn't she call my cell phone?" he challenged.

"Who knows? Do you have any witnesses to you being here all night?"

Spider's eyes averted them as he grappled for an answer. "I don't think so," he said unconvincingly.

Ohlemacher and Moore noticed his evasiveness.

"Are you sure?" Ohlemacher probed.

"I said no," Spider snapped.

"If you do think of anyone, let me know," Ohlemacher suggested.

"Sure. I'll do that," Spider agreed. He was anxious to get the two of them out of his house.

The two visitors left.

"He was squirming," Moore offered as they paused outside.

"I noticed that, too."

After leaving Spider, they spotted Hoover working in his backyard.

"Hello Henry," Ohlemacher called.

Hoover stood and adjusted his spectacles on his face. "Hello boys. What brings you two here? Have you found Elke?"

"That's the reason we're here," Ohlemacher announced. "Did you get a call on your cell phone from her late Labor Day night?"

"Yes, although I didn't know it was from her until the next morning."

"I don't understand," Moore interjected.

"Ada has a rule. If the phone rings after we go to bed, we don't answer it," Henry explained.

"Don't you even look at it to see who called?" Moore pushed.

"No. That makes Ada angry and you don't want to make her angry. You have no idea what it's like when she's mad." Hoover had a fearful look.

Such a milquetoast, Moore thought. The guy always had a meekness about him that made him an easy pushover.

"But you did listen to the message?" Ohlemacher asked.

"I did. First thing when I got up yesterday morning. I still have it on my cell phone. You want to hear it?" he asked nervously.

"Yes."

Hoover's fingers maneuvered the keypad and it played her slurred message.

"Henry, it's Elke. I hate to bother you and Ada, but could

you get your boat and pick me up? I'm behind the Overboard Bar on their dock in the Portage River. Please hurry."

"What did you do?" Ohlemacher asked.

"When I got up that morning, I checked my voicemail and heard her message. I called her to see if she was okay and didn't get an answer. So I took my boat over there."

"Was she there?"

"No. I tied up and walked down the path to the Overboard. It was closed. I didn't see her, so I headed back here."

Moore probed. "Did you notice anything suspicious here that night, Henry?"

"Now that you mention it. I couldn't fall back to sleep. I kind of tossed and turned. Getting waked out of a deep sleep by a ringing phone can get your heart racing. I remember one time . . ."

"Tell us what you noticed," Moore pressed.

"I heard Spider's boat start. You can't miss that rumble from its engine. I didn't think anything more about it until you just made me recall it," Hoover explained.

"Henry, why didn't you tell us about the phone message from Elke?" Moore grilled the man.

"It just slipped my mind. I'm sorry. I want to do whatever I can to help."

"It's the details, Henry, that can make a difference. I need you to be thinking better about details when we ask you questions," Ohlemacher interjected in a serious tone.

"I'm sorry."

"Thanks Henry. If anything else comes to mind, give me a call," Ohlemacher said as he and Moore began walking away.

"Back to Spider's?" Moore asked.

"You're getting good at this, Emerson," the chief smiled.

"Speaking of forgetting, I forgot to tell you that there was an incoming call the next morning to Elke's phone from Henry's phone in her phone records. That ties into his explanation."

Moore nodded his head at hearing the information.

They walked up the porch and knocked. About thirty seconds later, Spider appeared on the other side of the screen door.

"What is it now?" he asked gruffly.

"You mentioned that you were passed out and didn't hear Elke's message until the next morning," Ohlemacher stated.

"Right. Why?"

"Are you sure you didn't take your boat out and go get her?"

"I told you I was passed out."

"You didn't answer my question. Yes, or no?" Ohlemacher demanded.

"No," Spider snapped angrily.

"We have a report that your boat went out late Monday night shortly after Elke's call was placed."

"Hogwash! I was passed out," he stormed indignantly. Spider then saw Rio Hawkins emerge from the nearby public beach area. He was pushing his overflowing grocery cart.

"Ask our resident homeless man. He usually sleeps on the beach. Maybe he can tell you that my boat didn't go out Monday night."

"Hey Rio. Can you come over here," Ohlemacher called as he motioned for Hawkins to cross the street.

Hawkins acted as if he hadn't heard them and continued to walk barefoot down the sidewalk.

"Rio. I need you to come over here," Ohlemacher called in a stern voice.

"I'll go get him," Moore offered as he bounded down the

porch steps and over to Hawkins.

"Come on over, Rio. The chief wants to ask you something." Moore treated Hawkins with a quiet respect as he helped him across the street.

"I didn't do nothing," Hawkins mumbled as he cringed from Moore.

"There's nothing to worry about, Rio. The chief just has a couple of questions for you."

Hawkins looked sideways at Moore. He wasn't buying it.

"Rio, thanks for coming over," Ohlemacher said softly as he walked down the steps and approached Hawkins.

Hawkins didn't reply. He just looked from each man up to the porch where Spider was hostilely glaring at him. Hawkins looked away, intimidated. His face was a passive reflection of a traumatic past. His emotional countenance was that of a man who society had abandoned.

"Rio," the chief started, "did you see Spider's boat go out in the middle of the night Monday?"

"I see things," Hawkins murmured under his pungent breath.

"Did you see Spider's boat go out?" the chief repeated his question.

Hawkins turned his head to look at Spider once more. Spider's hateful, sadistic stare was as clear a warning as a drawn sword.

"I go now," he muttered as he turned to leave.

Moore watched Hawkins' eyes. He saw the pain in them, a lifetime of emotional scarring.

Moore then asked with a concerned tone, "Rio, did you see Spider's boat go out on Labor Day night?"

Shaking his head from side to side as he plodded away.

"No."

"I guess you'll believe me now," Spider boasted with an evil smirk.

"Hey Spider, I have a question for you," Moore called.

"What?" Spider growled.

"Did you have life insurance on Elke?"

"Emerson, not yet," Ohlemacher cautioned Moore as he put his hand on Moore's arm.

"I don't have anything to hide, Tom. Yes, I do. I have a $100,000 policy on her," he answered in a defiant tone. "Who doesn't have life insurance on their spouse? She has a policy on me, too," he bellowed.

Moore nodded as Ohlemacher spoke, "We've taken enough of your time. We'll be on our way."

Spider turned and went inside, allowing the door to slam behind him.

"Something's fishy if you ask me," Moore said as they headed to Ohlemacher's car. Rio was already crossing the street and heading back to the beach.

"Rio did not want to talk in front of Spider. That's for sure. We'll catch up with him later and see what he has to say," Ohlemacher noted.

"Why didn't you want me to ask about the life insurance?"

"I'd rather wait until we find out if we have a homicide. Right now, all we have is a missing person. I'm going to drop you at the dock so you can catch the *Sonny S* over to Middle Bass. I want you to find out more from Eddie. Think you can do that?"

"Sure."

"I'm going back to my office and put out a missing persons bulletin to area law enforcement and on social media with Elke's photo. Let's see if that helps us find her."

"Sounds like a plan," Moore said as Ohlemacher pulled to a stop by the *Sonny S* dock. Moore stepped out of the vehicle and headed for the ferry.

Forty minutes later, Moore was walking through the front door of the Middle Bass Island General Store.

"Is Eddie around?" he asked Bill Lodermeier.

"He's out back. You want me to get him for you, Emerson?"

"No. I'll just go out there and talk to him. Thanks Bill."

Moore walked through the building to the back door and exited. He spotted Sheller by his pickup truck.

"Hey Eddie."

"Hello Emerson. It just seems like any time I turn around, I spot you."

"And that's a good thing?"

"Depends," Sheller grinned.

"When you were at the Overboard Monday night, did you go over on your boat?"

"No. I drove my truck over on the ferry. Why?"

Moore continued. "Did you have any other exchanges with Elke?"

"No."

"Did you take her anywhere?"

"No. I told you that I helped her get out of the trunk. The last I saw her was when she headed down the path to the dock. I would assume she was having someone pick her up. Why all these questions?" he asked perplexed.

"It just seems like we've run into a series of people not telling us everything they know about her disappearance."

Sheller got really serious. "Emerson, you know me. I help people. I don't cause drama. If I didn't mention something to you, it's because I forgot. I'm not involved in any way with her disappearance other than what I've told you."

"Sorry Eddie. I don't mean to come across like I don't trust you. Tom and I are very frustrated that we can't find her."

"I gather that. I would be, too, if I was in your shoes."

The men chatted for another twenty minutes before Moore left to catch the ferry back to Put-in-Bay. When he landed, he walked to the police station to report to the chief.

After hearing Moore, Ohlemacher commented, "Another dead end."

"An epidemic of dead ends if you ask me," Moore replied. "Did you get a chance to send out your bulletin?"

"Yes. It went to police departments within a hundred-mile radius. I had Karen make several posts to social media. We'll see what turns up."

"I'm going to call it a night and head home," Moore sighed. It had been a long and unproductive day.

"Me too. I've got a couple of things I want to do first, but I'll be out of here shortly," Ohlemacher said as Moore walked out of his office.

CHAPTER 15

Next Morning
Middle Bass Island

Much of the island remained rather quiet. A lawn mower could faintly be heard in the distance. A middle-aged man in shorts and collared shirt was unloading several packages from a large brown van parked in front of a small cottage. A young girl was slowly riding her bicycle in circles near the park. The skies over Lake Erie were crystal clear as a cool September breeze bit at the leaves in the trees and tousled the landscaped flowers and shrubs.

In the office of Put-In-Bay police chief Tom Ohlemacher, the nearly quiet atmosphere was interrupted.

"Tom," his dispatcher Karen Ross summoned from down the hall.

"Yes, Karen?"

"You have a call on line one."

As he reached for the phone, the chief motioned for Emerson Moore to stay seated where he was. "Hello, Chief Ohlemacher speaking."

"Tom, it's Dave Nostrant."

"Hi Dave. Are you keeping everyone in line on Middle Bass?" the chief teased.

Nostrant cut to the chase. "Tom, Mike Gora and I were driving through the park and we had a couple of kids run up to us. They were wide-eyed and excited."

"Go on."

"You know where Riley Bostle's place is?"

"Yes. Just east of the old Lonz Winery boathouse," Ohlemacher replied as he pictured in his mind the stone boathouse built into the side of the hill with a dock in front of it.

"You know where they stacked those cars from the 1950s to stop shoreline erosion? Those old junker cars?"

"Yes. Some of them have trees growing through them," the chief acknowledged.

"The kids found a body sticking halfway in the water and halfway in one of the cars."

Ohlemacher's countenance abruptly changed at hearing the news. In a very serious tone he asked, "Did you or anyone there touch the body?"

"No. Mike made sure of that. We knew you wouldn't want any evidence disturbed."

"Do you have the kids with you?"

"Yes. They're sitting in Mike's truck and he's talking to them. They're partially excited about finding a body and upset at the same time."

"Did you climb down and check the body?"

"We went down, but didn't touch the body. It looked like it had been there for some time. It was face down and has blonde hair. It could be Elke."

"Stay where you are. Emerson and I will be right over."

"Will do."

As Ohlemacher hung up, he stood. "Come on Emerson. Dave Nostrant and Mike Gora are on Middle Bass with two kids who found a body along the shoreline."

"What? Do you think it's Elke's?"

"That's what they guess. I'll tell you everything on the way. We'll take the police boat over, and I need to call the coroner and forensic team to come out."

The two men scurried out of the office and drove to where the police boat was docked. Fifteen minutes later, they tied up the boat to the dock in front of the Lonz boathouse. They climbed the steep bank and quickly spotted the group waiting for them.

"That was fast," Gora said as he greeted the chief and Emerson.

"Where's the body?" Ohlemacher asked. He was totally focused. Mysterious deaths, including homicides, were very rare in the western basin of Lake Erie. What Ohlemacher felt in his gut was that he had a homicide on his hands to investigate. It was not how he envisioned approaching the end of the summer tourist season.

"Over there," Nostrant pointed into the near distance close to the Lonz boat dock where Ohlemacher and Moore had just arrived.

The chief and Moore walked over with Gora to the top of the bank and peered down toward the water at the row of discarded cars lining the hillside as an erosion barrier.

"It's the second car in," Gora explained.

Ohlemacher assessed the steepness of the bank. "We're going to have to be careful here, Emerson," he said as he stepped cautiously down the slope, grabbing onto nearby trees for support. Moore carefully followed him, while Gora remained behind.

When they reached the waterline, they entered the lake and waded around the first car.

"There," Ohlemacher pointed.

As Nostrant had described, they saw a fully-clothed body. It was Elke White.

"The body is bloated. That tells me it's been here for a while," the chief said as his eyes scanned the body. "I see what looks like blunt force trauma to the left side of the head. There's some blood there."

"Think that's from the fall at the Overboard Bar?" Moore asked as he peered at the body.

"Could be."

"Did she drown?"

"I don't think so, Emerson. She's not in the drowning position."

In reaction to the perplexed look on Moore's face, Ohlemacher explained, "That's when the extremities and head are hanging downward toward the bottom while the individual's back is toward the surface. She's more stretched out. And I don't see any postmortem abrasions on her hands or forehead. She still has her shoes on. She was killed somewhere else and dumped here. That's my guess."

The chief looked up the bank. "I don't think she was dragged down the bank. The only disturbance on the bank that I saw on our way down here was from the two kids who we need to talk to."

Ohlemacher looked at how the body was draped partially inside the doorless vehicle. He turned his head and his eyes examined the shore which was a mixture of sand and stones. "And I don't see any evidence of a boat grounding itself here, at least recently. The ebb and flow of the lake would cause any marks to be filled in."

The chief waded out several steps more into the lake up to his knees and looked around.

Joining him, Moore asked, "What are you looking for?"

"Anything out of the ordinary."

Moore looked across the open water at South Bass Island. "You can see the back of the Spider's Web B&B from here," Moore observed.

"I know. And do you know whose house is on top of the hill above us here?"

"Riley Bostle?"

"Right."

"Pretty convenient," Moore commented.

"Possibly very telling. Or maybe someone wants us to believe that she's involved. Could be a setup."

Ohlemacher surveyed the area for another minute. "I don't see anything here. Let's go up top and talk to the kids."

The two men made their way out of the water and back to the top of the bank where Ohlemacher produced a roll of yellow police tape to cordon off the area. Moore helped him.

They next turned their attention to questioning the two young boys. The ten-year-olds had been spending a few days camping nearby with their parents when they decided to go exploring.

Finishing with the boys, the chief had them sit nearby while he further questioned Nostrant and Gora. Not getting any additional revelations from them, Ohlemacher turned to Moore and said, "Let's walk these boys over to their parents and explain to them what they stumbled across."

"Sure."

Ohlemacher addressed the two lads. "I'm proud of you both, that was a tough thing to see. You know, courage is an odd thing. You never know when or how you might find it. You will always wonder if you'll have courage the day you need it most. You boys showed that courage today, for sure. Thank you."

He and Moore then walked the two boys back to their families and explained to them what had transpired. The parents were horrified, but chose to remain on the island. Having attained their respective contact information, Ohlemacher and Moore returned to the top of the hill.

"There's the coroner," the chief said as he spotted a police boat approaching the dock. After they arrived, he talked with the coroner and forensic team for a few minutes.

"Come with me, Emerson," Ohlemacher directed as the coroner and forensic team headed down the bank to examine the corpse.

"Where are we going?"

"We're paying a visit to Riley Bostle. I want to see her reaction when we tell her who we found and ask her some questions."

"You think she did it?"

"Don't know. But being Spider's mistress and the location of the body makes her a person of interest," Ohlemacher noted as the two walked toward Bostle's house.

The chief knocked on the front door, then heard a voice call, "I'll be right there." A few moments later, Bostle opened the door and walked onto the porch. "What brings a police officer to my door?" she asked with a suspicious look on her face.

"Riley, we haven't met. I'm . . ."

"I know who you are, Chief, and I also know the person with you. Now, what do you two want with me?" she asked with an annoyed tone.

"You do know Spider White?" Ohlemacher asked.

"Yes. What about it?" she snapped.

"I assume you know that his wife has disappeared."

Frowning with exasperation at being asked, she replied,

"Yes. I heard. Everyone on the islands have heard. What of it?"

"I'll get to that in a moment. Late in the night after Labor Day, did you hear any noise coming from the bank where the erosion barrier is, or maybe from the Lonz boathouse?"

"No. I was sleeping. I wouldn't have heard anything anyway because of the noise from my window air conditioner in my bedroom. What's this all about?" she barked.

Ohlemacher ignored her question. "So you wouldn't have heard a vehicle pull over by the edge of the cliff and park or a boat dock below the bank?"

"No. I just explained how noisy my air conditioner is," she cracked with anger.

"Have you seen Elke any time in the last week?"

Bostle's eyes caught the yellow police tape in the near distance on the edge of the bank. "Did you find her body?" she asked. "Is that what this is all about?"

Moore's eyebrows shot up at her question.

"No one said anything about a body, Riley. Why did you?" Ohlemacher probed.

"If she's missing, I'd just figure she'd be dead. Is that why you're asking me all of these questions? You think I'm involved? I'll tell you one thing and that is, if I was involved, I wouldn't be so stupid as to put her body in front of my house," she shrieked. "I'm done if you're done with me." She spat out her words with venom.

"We're done for now, but we may want you to come to the station at Put-in-Bay if we have more questions," Ohlemacher responded as she turned her back on the men. She walked away in a huff, allowing the door to slam shut behind her.

As the two men departed, Moore commented, "Interesting how she brought up a body in the conversation."

"Yeah. As did Spider. I noticed that, too. There's more behind this than she's letting on."

"I noticed that she didn't seem too shocked about Elke's body possibly being over the bank."

"Suspicious, isn't it?"

"I'll say," Emerson confirmed.

"I've got some things I want to do when we get back," Ohlemacher said as they headed for the police boat. "But first, we'll take a ride over to Spider's dock and inform him."

Meanwhile, Bostle was on the phone. She was screaming at Spider. "The police were just here. They found Elke's body. Why did you leave her body in front of my place? You idiot," she started before unloosing a chain of expletives at him. "Don't you know this will tie me into her murder plot? What were you thinking?" she stormed as she unleashed another fusillade of profanity at him.

When she paused to take a breath, Spider interjected, "It wasn't me. I'm not that stupid."

Before he could continue, she cut him off. "It wasn't you? How can you say that when it was part of our plan? Did you change the plan? What are you up to?" she raged.

"I'm telling you I didn't do it," Spider protested.

"I don't believe you. I think you're lying to me. You just want to keep the insurance money to yourself. You're trying to set me up to take the fall, aren't you?" she bristled.

"You need to simmer down," Spider said as he grappled with her eruption. "What did the police ask you? Do they suspect your involvement?"

"They wanted to know if I heard anything? You know how noisy that air conditioner is in my bedroom. I told them that I couldn't hear anything going on outside."

"They ask you anything else?"

"They wanted to know when was the last time I saw Elke. I knew where their questioning was headed and told them I wasn't stupid enough as to dump her body in front of my house."

"Did they ask anything about me?"

"Yeah. They asked if I knew you," she replied.

"Anything else about me?"

"No, but I bet they'll stop by to see you today. You better have your story straight," she warned.

Spider smiled calmly. "I'll be ready for them. They don't know who they're dealing with," he commented with an evil smirk on his face. "You calm down. It's all going to work out. Once I cash in the insurance policies and sell this dump, we'll be on our way," he assured her.

"You really mean that, Spider?" she asked, still not totally confident with his promises.

"Trust me."

That comment touched a nerve. "The last time a man told me to trust him, I got stuck with this house that needed so many repairs after he died."

"But don't forget Riley, that's what brought us together. It all started with me helping a widow."

Bostle recalled how the two met and his offer to repair her front door that wasn't locking properly. "I guess," she said as her blood pressure started dropping.

"It's all going to work out. We'll head to Florida and enjoy life. Just the two of us."

"Okay. You be careful with Tom Ohlemacher and you better fess up to me about killing Elke."

"We'll talk more," Spider said as he skillfully put her off. "One more thing, Riley. Everyone is going to be watching us.

These two islands have a lot of eyes. We better not be seen together for a while," he cautioned.

"What?"

"Other than me sneaking over in the middle of the night to make my visit with you. But you'll have to check and make sure that I can still tie up at that old boathouse."

"Okay. Are you coming over tonight?" she asked.

"Not tonight, but soon. We have to be extra careful. And you be careful what you say to people"

"I will."

"I'm the most likely suspect and I need to play this out well," Spider cautioned her in a firm tone.

"Just be sure you don't get caught. That would blow everything," she countered as they ended the call.

The police boat soon arrived at the dock to the east of Spider's Web B&B. Moore and the chief secured the craft and walked over to the house where they found Spider sitting on the front porch, calmly sipping a beer.

"Good morning," Ohlemacher began slowly as they walked up the steps and stood in front of Spider.

Spider looked up at the men. "What brings you here again? Do you have any news on Elke?" he asked with feigned concern.

"I'm sorry, Spider. We found her. She's not with us anymore."

"What?" he asked in mock disbelief.

"Her body has been found," Moore interjected as he closely watched Spider's reaction.

Moore and Ohlemacher each suspected that Bostle had called Spider immediately after they questioned her to inform him that Elke's body was found. They also believed Bostle tipped off Spider that they were on their way to again question him about his wife's death.

Spider's countenance changed as he feigned a numbing look of sorrow on his face. "I'll need to make funeral arrangements. Where's her corpse?"

"It's on its way to the morgue for an autopsy. We will let you know when the funeral home can pick it up. Probably in a few days," Ohlemacher answered.

Spider stood. "If you don't mind, I'm going inside. This is quite a shock," he said as he played his part. Not waiting for a reply, he walked inside the house, letting the door bang shut behind him.

Moore and the chief exchanged glances.

"He's really upset," Moore said sarcastically.

"I've seen better acting from my first-grade grandson," Ohlemacher added.

"Suspect #1?"

"I'd guess so," Ohlemacher replied as they walked back to the dock.

"Did you notice he didn't ask where her body was found or how she died?"

"Very good, Emerson. I'm pleased that you noticed that."

"I bet Riley called him and told him what she knew," Moore offered.

"I wouldn't be surprised."

"Think they are in cahoots?" Moore asked.

"It would appear that way. Let's take the boat back and return to my office. I've got an idea."

Forty-five minutes later, the men were in Ohlemacher's office. The chief was standing next to a white board where he wrote _'Suspect.'_ Underneath the word, he wrote Spider's name, then listed three column headings: _'Motive,'_ _'Means'_ and _'Op-_

portunity.'

"Let's start with listing potential suspects. Any others besides Spider?" he asked.

"Riley Bostle?"

"Right. Who else?"

"Braxton," Moore suggested.

Ohlemacher listed the name. "Anybody else?"

Moore thought a moment. "Henry Hoover? Elke called him to pick her up."

"Yes. Anyone else?" He was interested in seeing how Moore's ideas matched his own.

Moore bowed his head in deeper thought. Looking up, he suggested, "Rio Hawkins?"

"Maybe, but he wasn't the one I was thinking about," Ohlemacher responded as he added the name to the growing list.

"Who were you thinking?"

"You're not going to like this one, Emerson. Eddie Sheller." Ohlemacher then wrote Sheller's name on the whiteboard.

"Eddie?" Moore was stunned.

"Yes. We know that he was the last one on record to see her alive."

"I don't believe it," Moore protested.

"We need to go through the drill. If we can eliminate him, we will. But we've got to add him. Let's look at the motive column. Spider and Riley were having an affair. They most likely would like to see Elke out of the picture."

"Right and I'd say they are our prime suspects," Moore agreed.

"Braxton has lied to us. I think there's more there than we know."

"Right and Hoover could be the rejected lover, if that."

"Very good, Emerson. What about Rio?"

"I'm not sure. He seemed to like her. But he doesn't have a boat to take her body over to dump it."

"Correct and that belongs in the 'Means' column. What about Eddie?" Ohlemacher probed.

"You've got me there. He's such a good guy," Moore replied. He was stymied by that name being added on the list.

"He knew her. Was she ever involved with him and no one knew? You take a guy like him with movie star good looks and women chasing him. We've got to check him out more."

Moore shook his head from side to side. "I'm having a difficult time with Eddie being included."

"I know you are, Emerson, but bear with me."

Just then the door opened and Cranston walked in. "Uncle Tommy, I just heard that you found Elke's corpse." As he spoke, his eyes found their way to the whiteboard. "I see you're way ahead of me. I was going to suggest a list of suspects for you, Uncle Tommy," he said as he studied the list of names.

Ohlemacher groaned inwardly at his nephew walking in on them. He didn't want him involved. He decided to humor Cranston. "Are we missing anyone?" he asked reluctantly.

"Naw. You did a pretty good job of listing the right people," Cranston said pompously.

"I didn't know you had experience investigating murder cases, A.C.," Moore commented.

"Oh yeah. I have experience. Once, I solved a serial murder case," Cranston stated proudly as he rubbed his right hand under his left armpit.

"I didn't know that," Ohlemacher commented. "Tell us about it."

"I don't like to brag, but I did all of the work. Yessiree. I caught the killer red-handed," Cranston said without explaining.

"I never heard anything about it. Tell us, A.C.," Ohlemacher pushed.

Cranston rocked back and forth on his heels. "Well, it was really nothing, Uncle Tommy." He still did not reveal what had transpired.

"Come on A.C., tell us what happened," Moore pleaded.

Cranston looked around to be sure that no one was within hearing distance before whispering. "We've got to keep this real quiet. It happened in Toledo. I was checking an alley behind a furniture store when I saw the big door on the delivery dock open. That's when I saw a man beating the life out of Franklin. He had a sledge hammer and was slamming Franklin. I pulled over and ran to rescue Franklin, but I was too late. Franklin was gone."

"Did you take the culprit into custody?" Ohlemacher asked.

"Yes. I took him down to the station. He protested the entire time. Then they released him because he owned the furniture store."

"Why?"

"No one was there to press charges."

Moore cocked his head as he stared at Cranston. "A.C., would the Franklin you mentioned be a Franklin recliner?"

Cranston's face turned beet red. "I need to quit jawing and get back to work," he stammered as he quickly exited the office.

Ohlemacher shook his head from side to side. "Not sure what I'm going to do with that nephew of mine." He returned his attention to the whiteboard. "I think we can agree that everyone we listed except Rio has the means in which to commit a murder."

"Right," Moore agreed as he studied the whiteboard.

"And I'd think they all would have a motive and opportunity."

"Right," Moore agreed again although he wasn't convinced about Sheller having a motive.

"We're going to have to dig deeper."

The two kicked around several theories before calling it a night. But before they left, Cranston had returned to Ohlemacher's office.

"Aliens got her if you ask me," Cranston interjected.

Moore groaned despite himself as he gave Ohlemacher a forlorn look. He was not excited about Cranston becoming involved in investigating Elke's death. Neither was Ohlemacher.

"Yep aliens. There've been some sightings here," Cranston rattled on. "I found a couple out at Oak Point in the middle of the night. They were under a blanket. I sneaked up on them and pulled off their blanket and they were naked. They told me aliens stole their clothes. That's why they were naked under the blanket. Lucky I showed up when I did because the aliens probably saw me coming and dropped their clothes. I told them to get dressed while I stood guard."

"That was really good of you to have saved them," Ohlemacher feigned amazement.

"Aw shucks, Uncle Tommy. It was nothing."

"Did you see the aliens, A.C.?" Moore asked as he played along.

"No. Must have been some of them invisible ones. You run into that kind every once in a while," Cranston explained pompously as he rubbed his left armpit with his right hand. "There's been a rash of alien sightings recently."

"Oh?" Ohlemacher asked.

"I caught Rio Hawkins dumpster diving behind Frosty's. He told me that he was looking for aliens."

"He did?" Ohlemacher asked with mock disbelief.

"Yessiree. He's told me he's seen stuff happening at night when he's been sleeping on the public beach. They wake him up with all the noise."

The comment caught Moore's attention. "What kind of things? Did he say?"

"No. You can hardly get the man to talk and when he does, he mumbles. We really need to run him to some homeless shelter, Uncle Tommy."

"He won't stay. People have tried that for several months."

"This Elke thing sounds like something where you need my investigative prowess, Uncle Tommy. All I've been dealing with are things like a lady who lost her driver's license and a boater who said someone stole his cooler off his boat. I need something with some meat on it that requires my skill," Cranston complained.

"I'd expect you to keep to your business at hand. Emerson and I are handling the matter with Elke. I'll let you know if you are needed," Ohlemacher advised his nephew.

"But Uncle Tommy, I can really help you. Let me help," Cranston pleaded.

"Just do your job and keep your eyes open. That's what I need you to do. If I need you to join the missing persons team, I'll let you know," the chief said quietly.

Cranston hung his head with disappointment as he walked out of the chief's office.

CHAPTER 16

The Next Morning
Doorbell Inn

Moore had arrived late morning to pay a visit to his aunt. They were seated on the front porch under a darkening sky that forewarned of a coming storm. The wind had picked up, swirling and scattering leaves and small debris through the air.

"Looks like we're in for a bad storm," Aunt Anne mused as her eyes went from the approaching black clouds to the angry waves pounding the breakwall.

"Sure does," Moore agreed as he watched the trees bend in the stiffening wind and the seagrass wands sway by the public beach.

"I heard about Elke," she said quietly.

"Word gets around fast," Moore observed.

"It's the island grapevine," she murmured. "Do they know who killed her? Was it Spider?" she asked as she stared at the house next door.

"Aunt Anne, you know that I can't say anything," Moore answered.

"Because you're helping with the investigation, right?"

"You got it." Moore was glad that she understood.

The door opened and Ada walked through it. She walked in front of them and looked at Moore. "Did you guys lock up Spider yet?"

Moore allowed a smile to cross his face. "No one has been locked up."

"He should be. I heard he bought a $350,000 life insurance policy on Elke two weeks ago."

"What?" Moore asked, stunned. "How do you know?"

"Henry told me this morning when he heard that Elke was murdered."

"How does Henry know?"

"He probably overheard Spider and that hussy Riley talking. Spider is not a soft-talking man. You hear a lot, especially when the window to his office is open." Ada pointed to the rear of Spider's house.

Moore stood and peered around the corner. The two houses were thirty feet apart and separated by the Doorbell Inn driveway. He could see the open window to Spider's first floor office.

"You can see his place extends farther back than ours. So, when Henry is in our backyard, he can hear stuff. And let me tell you, you don't have to be in the backyard when Spider loses his temper. The screaming and shouting probably can be heard all the way to the chamber office. I've had some of our guests complain about it."

"Did you say anything to Spider about the complaints?" Moore asked.

"It's like talking to a wall. He just gets mad and yells at Henry or me when we brought them up. We talked to Elke, but she said she couldn't do anything about it. He's a madman. The sooner you guys quit wasting time and lock him up, the better!" Ada said firmly.

"I bet," Moore said.

"I've got to get back to work," she said as she turned and entered the inn.

"She certainly doesn't think highly of Spider," Moore commented quietly to his aunt.

"No. And she'd like to see him go to jail," Aunt Anne noted.

"Why? Because he's an unruly neighbor and may have killed Elke?" Moore questioned.

"Yes, but's there's more. Ada wants to buy that house. She told me she could do a better job running it as a B&B."

"Really?" Moore reacted as he thought whether Ada should be added to the suspect list.

Before either could speak, the air was filled with thunder like a drumroll and the crack of lightning striking nearby. The wind gusted and brought along a sheet of driving rain that was rapidly moving toward them off the lake.

"I better be going," Moore said as he started down the stairs. He noticed Hawkins' grocery cart covered by a tarp. It was parked on the other side of the porch. "Is Rio here?" he asked from the sidewalk.

"No. Henry lets him park his grocery cart here when he goes off wandering on Delaware Avenue," Aunt Anne explained. "You better get in your car. Here it comes," she warned as the rain started pelting Moore.

Moore raced to his car and jumped in as the storm on its way west unleashed its fury on the island. He started his car and drove down a nearly deserted street with his windshield wipers fighting a losing battle to clear the windshield. As he neared the merry-go-round, he spotted a half-bent over figure walking barefooted in the cold downpour. It was Rio Hawkins.

Moore pulled over and lowered his window. "Rio, get in here. I'll give you a ride."

Sheets of heavy droplets had drenched Hawkins, clinging to his skin to form a cold sheen and plastering his greying hair to his head. The wind cut through his clothes as if they weren't even there, so thin and worn were they. Even then, he tightly held his worn jacket closed.

Hawkins recognized Moore, but shook his head negatively and waved for Moore to move on.

Moore ignored it. "Come on Rio. You're soaking wet. Get in and let's get you warmed up."

Hawkins hesitated, then moved around the car and joined Moore in his protective, dry comfort. His breath stank as he mumbled a "thank you."

Moore looked at the wet, shoeless vagrant. His leathery feet and face were turning blue from the cold.

"Let me turn the heater on," Moore offered as he reached for the controls. The blast of hot air comforted Hawkins, who nodded his head in appreciation.

Spotting Pasquale's restaurant ahead, Moore had an idea. "Rio, I was just on my way to grab lunch. Why don't you join me? My treat and it will give you a chance to dry off."

Hawkins shook his head negatively. "I don't want to be a bother," he muttered quietly.

"Rio, you are no bother. Come on. It will be fun for me to sit with you and talk. You'd do me a favor."

Hawkins was surprised at the offer. He was more used to people chasing him away. He turned his head and studied Moore for a moment. The offer of a hot meal was enticing. "I guess I could do that," he murmured.

"Excellent," Moore said as he turned left onto the street between the restaurant and the Park Hotel. He parked behind the restaurant and the two shared his umbrella as they walked to the entrance. They entered and found a table overlooking Delaware Avenue, DeRivera Park and the docks on the bay.

"We can enjoy watching the rain from here and be nice and dry."

"I'm going to use the bathroom," Hawkins mumbled as he started for the restrooms.

"Can I get you a coffee to start?"

Hawkins nodded as he shuffled away.

"Staying dry?" a voice asked.

Moore looked up and saw Ty Winchester, the gregarious restaurant manager, approaching his table. Moore had always admired him for his involvement in the island community. He was also one of the organizers for the island's successful Pyrate Fest each year.

"Trying."

"Was that Rio Hawkins with you?" Winchester asked.

"Yes. Poor guy. He was caught out in the rain."

"That's some cold rain to be caught in," Winchester observed.

"My exact thoughts. Poor guy was getting drenched in the rain. I pulled over and gave him a ride over here."

"Can I get you both coffees to warm you up?"

"That would be great for a starter, Ty," Moore answered.

Winchester walked away and Hawkins returned. It looked like he had dried off a bit while he was in the restroom. He shivered as he slipped off his thin coat and placed it on the back of the chair to dry out.

"I ordered coffee," Moore said as he watched the gaunt man sit.

No sooner had Moore spoken than Winchester returned with the two coffees. He set them down and handed Hawkins a sweatshirt. "Here Rio. You look wet and cold. Have one of the sweatshirts from Pyrate Fest. It's dry, and it'll help warm you up. No charge."

A look of astonishment crossed Hawkins' face as he muttered a "thank you." He took off his shirt, revealing his lean frame and quickly slipped on the sweatshirt. He allowed a small smile to show on his face.

"Ready to order?" Winchester asked.

Moore went first. "I'll take one of your famous ham and cheese omelets with hash browns and rye toast."

"Got it. Rio?"

"The same." Hawkins was a man of few words. He wasn't used to talking. He had lost the will to converse. Not many people would speak to someone as lowly as him. Still, he held a dying gleam of hope that his life would one day improve. He was a poor castoff, who would treasure some emotional warmth, even if only for a little while.

Moore studied Hawkins' weathered skin and skeletal face with its protruding cheekbones. It cried out with loneliness. Moore sensed the man needed reassurance and for someone to see his humanity.

"Are you warmer?" Moore asked.

Hawkins averted his gaze, not meeting Moore's friendly eyes. The harshness of street life taught him very quickly to stay isolated in every possible way, even a stray glance could mean trouble.

Moore asked again. "Are you warmer, Rio?"

Hawkins nodded his head as he looked at the downpour outside amidst claps of thunder and flashes of lightning.

"Rio, it's okay to talk to me. You're safe talking to me. I'm pretty easy to get along with," Moore said in a soothing, friendly tone as he sought to make Hawkins comfortable with him.

"Thanks."

"I am. I really am," Moore reassured him.

"I know."

Moore realized that the man wasn't going to open up easily.

Winchester reappeared with their meals and set them down on the table. Hawkins picked up his fork and ravished his plate, finishing before Moore was halfway through his meal. When the couple at the table next to them left, Hawkins walked over and picked up their two pieces of leftover pepperoni pizza and brought them back to the table. He quickly devoured them, emitted a large burp and sat back to enjoy his coffee.

When Winchester returned to refresh their coffee, Moore whispered to him before he walked away. Moore took his last bite and looked at Hawkins. "Was that good?"

Hawkins' eyes glanced briefly at Moore. "Yes. Thank you."

Moore remembered Cranston's comment about Hawkins saying that he saw things. He decided to pursue it.

"Rio, did you hear that Elke White was found dead on Middle Bass Island?"

With widened eyes and a noticeable change in his mood, Hawkins replied sadly, "No."

"She was a good lady," Moore said to see if Hawkins would say anything.

"She was kind to me," Hawkins commented dismally.

Moore decided to continue to see if anything of value would be disclosed.

"Did you ever hear her and Spider argue?"

Hawkins didn't respond at first, causing Moore to repeat his question.

"Did you ever hear her and Spider argue?"

Hawkins nodded.

"Did you ever see Spider strike her?"

Hawkins nodded again. "I don't like him."

"Why?"

"He's mean."

"Was he mean to you?"

Hawkins didn't answer right away. He was struggling with what to say. "Yes."

"Did he harm you?"

"Yes."

"How?"

"He's chased me with a knife and a bat."

"Did he catch you?"

"No. She would stop him. I can't run fast. My feet . . ."

He didn't finish.

"Rio, I understand that you see things. What kind of things do you see?"

Hawkins' facial appearance shifted as his brow creased and tension ensued. He clammed up.

Moore saw the abrupt change and wondered what Hawkins didn't want to share. "Did you see something that involved Spider seriously hurting Elke?" Moore pushed.

In reaction, Hawkins stared at his plate. "I'm ready to go."

Lightning struck nearby with a loud crack. "I think I should drive you somewhere. Where can I take you?"

"The Chamber of Commerce office."

"Are you planning on staying under the covered area to wait out the storm?"

"Yes."

"I've got somewhere better for you. I'll take you to the Doorbell Inn and treat you to a room for the night. You can take a shower, relax, watch some TV and get warmed up. The storm should be well gone by morning. How does that sound to you?"

It took a second or two for Moore's incredibly kind offer

to sink in. Hawkins felt his lips stretch wide into a grin and his eyebrows arched for the sky. "Thank you."

"You are welcome. I'm going to pay the bill," Moore said as he stood. "I'll be right back."

When Moore returned, he was carrying a large flat box which he handed to Hawkins. "I noticed how much you enjoyed that pepperoni pizza. So, I ordered you one. You can munch on it while you watch TV," Moore smiled.

"Thank you," Hawkins said as he stood and took the box. He wasn't used to be treated kindly. He followed Moore out the back door and they drove over to the inn. Moore explained to Ada and his aunt what he was doing and, as luck would have it, there was an unoccupied room available.

When Moore started to leave, Hawkins grabbed him by the arm. "Thank you. This is so kind of you."

Moore smiled as he realized that was the most he ever heard Hawkins say. "No problem. And please remember to let me know if you want to tell me about the things you've seen. Ada or my aunt can get me for you."

Hawkins nodded.

Moore ran out of the house through the drenching rain to his car and drove to the police station to update the chief about the additional life insurance policy that Spider took out on Elke.

"That's interesting if it's true," Ohlemacher said as Moore finished bringing him up to speed, including his lunch with Rio Hawkins.

"Makes you wonder why Spider didn't reveal the additional $350,000 life insurance policy," Moore stated.

"And possibly explains why Spider has been pestering me for a copy of the death certificate," Ohlemacher added.

"I didn't realize he was," Moore reacted.

"Daily phone calls . . . Henry Hoover's name is sure coming up a lot lately."

"Yes. I noticed that, too."

Ohlemacher examined a map of the island affixed to his office wall as he contemplated. Turning to Moore, he asked, "Did you get a chance to check out Eddie?"

"No. I had planned on going today, but this storm changed my plans. I'll go over tomorrow."

CHAPTER 17

The Next Afternoon
Middle Bass Island

Moore had spent most of the day visiting with island residents. During the conversations he casually would mention Eddie's name to see what kind of reaction he would get. Not a person spoke ill of him. It was obvious he was highly thought of. Moore was even more convinced that Sheller wasn't involved.

As he boarded the *Sonny S* for his return trip to Put-in-Bay, he saw Riley Bostle seated and decided to sit across from her.

Bostle eyed him suspiciously. "There's plenty of empty seats. You don't have to sit across from me," she snapped.

"I know, Riley, but it gives me a chance to talk with you," Moore replied nonchalantly.

Bostle frowned in reaction and started to get up to sit elsewhere.

"No. Please don't, Riley," Moore urged. "Stay here."

"Why?"

"You don't have anything to hide, do you? Is that why you wanted to move?" Moore questioned calmly.

"No." Bostle stated as she plopped back down in her seat. "What do you want to talk about?" She decided she needed to throw off any suspicions that he may have about her involvement in Elke's death.

"You know there's a rumor about you and Spider having an affair, right?" Moore confronted her head-on.

"I don't have time for rumors. Rumormongers should direct

their energies somewhere else," she rebuked as she glared with emotional indifference.

"Stuff like that happens when they see a married man visiting your home."

"Oh, for crying out loud! Spider's a wonderful man who tries to help widows with small home repairs. He should be commended," she said as her mood turned to passionately defend Spider. "And just so you know, Elke supported him helping me."

"How do you know?" Moore probed.

"He told me."

"Did Elke tell you?" Moore asked in disbelief.

"No. Just Spider."

"Were you and Elke close?"

"Not really. I've stopped by their place from time to time. We would chat briefly when she was there," she explained.

Moore noted her answer indicated that Elke was not always present when she visited their residence.

"I'd stop by with fresh baked goods for Spider to show my appreciation for my home repairs," she added.

Moore wanted to ask if she showed her appreciation in any other way, but decided against it. "Are you going there now?"

"Yes. I want to express my condolences to Spider. Poor man. Losing his wife."

Moore nodded in agreement.

"Did you find the killer?" she asked.

"Not yet. But we're closing in," Moore said as he watched her reaction closely.

"Who did it?"

"Can't say."

"Who do you think did it?" she pushed.

"That's not for public consumption," Moore replied.

"Doesn't that make you special, having little secrets that you can't tell?" she barked with a cold emptiness and a complete disregard for Moore's professionalism.

She stood up. "I'm done talking with you, Mr. Moore." She walked away to take a seat near the stern of the ferry.

Moore shrugged his shoulders in response as the ferry neared its dock at The Boardwalk. Ten minutes later, Moore was seated in Ohlemacher's office, sharing the results of his investigation on Middle Bass Island and conversation with Riley Bostle.

"That Riley is a piece of work," Ohlemacher commented.

"I think she and Spider were in cahoots to murder Elke, take the insurance money and run," Moore offered.

"But it seems strange that Elke's body would be dumped in front of Riley's house. With the rumors about her affair with Spider, it doesn't fit. It's too obvious," Ohlemacher said a bit perplexed.

"And that may be part of their plan. Throw off everybody by taking an obvious step like that. They probably hope that it would lead investigators to think they weren't involved," Moore suggested.

"You could be right on that idea. We'll continue running down any lead we get. Thanks for checking out Eddie. I agree that he's not likely a top-tier suspect." The chief added, "There's a connection between the murderer and Elke like an umbilical cord of hate."

Moore nodded in agreement.

"I think I'll call it a day," Moore said as he headed for the door. He looked forward in returning to Warren's place and taking a break.

CHAPTER 18

The Next Day
Warren's Museum

Moore was enjoying his Sunday helping Warren with yard work when his cell phone rang. As he pulled it out of his pocket, he saw that the caller was Ohlemacher. So much for a day of solitude, Moore thought.

"Hi Tom," Moore answered.

"You busy?" Ohlemacher asked in a serious tone as he skipped the niceties and got to the point.

"I always have time for you," Moore said as he wiped his brow.

"We have another."

"Another?" Moore asked quizzically.

"Riley Bostle's body was discovered a few minutes ago. Same spot as Elke's."

"What?" Moore asked dumbfounded.

"The call just came in. Can you join me at the dock and we'll take the police boat over to Middle Bass?" Ohlemacher asked with a sense of urgency.

"Give me five minutes and I'll be on my way," Moore said as he ended the call.

"Trouble?" Warren asked when he read Moore's reactions.

"Yes. I'll tell you what I can when I get back," Moore said before racing into the house to wash up and change. In a few minutes, he was driving to the dock.

After he parked, he ran over to the police boat where the

chief instructed him. "Cast off the lines and jump aboard."

Moore did as instructed. When he boarded, he walked up to Ohlemacher at the helm.

"Can you tell me what you know?"

"Almost a replay of the discovery of Elke's body."

"What do you mean?"

"Dave Nostrant and Michael Gora found Riley and called me right away."

"What were they doing down there?"

"They were looking for clues that we may have missed when we recovered Elke's body."

A suspicious look appeared on Moore's face.

Ohlemacher noticed it. "What are you thinking?"

"Do you think they are involved with the murders? It seems strange that they were involved in discovering both bodies," Moore observed.

"Coincidence? I don't know," Ohlemacher surmised, "but we will question both of them and closely watch their reactions . . . You were on the *Sonny S* with Riley yesterday afternoon, right Emerson?"

"Right. Why?"

"And she told you that she was going to pay her respects to Spider, right?"

"Yes. She did. She was on her way to do just that when I spoke with her," Moore confirmed.

"Did she say anything about going anywhere else?"

Moore thought for a moment. "No. She only indicated that she was going to see him."

"Then Spider may have been the last one to see her alive," Ohlemacher concluded. "We'll need to question him. We will when we're finished on Middle Bass. He may be aware of where she planned to go after her visit with him."

Ohlemacher eased back on the throttle as they approached the dock by the Lonz boathouse. Moore jumped off the boat and secured the lines before the two walked over to where Nostrant and Gora were standing.

"Gentlemen," Ohlemacher greeted the two. "Where is she?"

"She's down there," Nostrant pointed.

"Did you touch the body?"

"I checked for a pulse, but couldn't find one," Gora answered.

"We didn't think she was alive. We noticed that her hands and lips were purple, and there was a waxen pallor to the skin," Nostrant added.

"You didn't disturb the area, right?"

"No. We were walking in the shallow water when we spotted her. Then we walked down a bit farther before climbing to the top of the bank."

"Okay. You two stay here. Emerson, let's walk over there where they climbed the bank. That way we won't disturb any possible clues."

"Okay," Moore agreed as he followed Ohlemacher down to the small beach and into the shallow water.

They walked over to the body, looking for any clues as they went. When they reached the body, Ohlemacher stopped and pointed. "Looks like stab wounds in the back," he noted.

Moore nodded as he looked around. "I don't see anything else."

"I don't either," Ohlemacher said. "The coroner and the forensic team from Port Clinton should be here shortly."

The two men waded through the shallow water, but didn't find any clues.

"You think Dave and Mike are involved?" Moore asked again.

"I don't, but let's go ask them some more questions," Ohlemacher directed as he headed back to the spot where they had descended. When they returned to the two men, Ohlemacher asked Nostrant to sit in his truck while they asked Gora a few questions. When they finished, Ohlemacher had Nostrant and Gora switch places.

While he and Moore were questioning Nostrant, they noticed the coroner and forensic team arrive in their boat. Ohlemacher paused his questioning long enough to point them to the body.

After finishing with Nostrant, Ohlemacher allowed him to leave with Gora.

"What do you think?" Moore asked. "Are they suspects?"

"No. Do you think they should be?"

"I don't. They just seem to have been at the right place at the wrong time. But it was good that they found the body," Moore observed.

"Yes, it was."

Ohlemacher, with Moore close behind, again walked to the edge of the bank. "Any early guesstimate on the cause of death?" the chief called down to the coroner, who was about to retrieve Bostle's body.

The coroner looked up from her examination of the body. "Yes. There are multiple stab wounds present on the back. It appears that one wound is through the right side of the thoracic aorta and through the right thoracic cavity. But we will know more when we complete an autopsy."

"I didn't notice any blood on the ground," Ohlemacher mentioned.

"We didn't either. There's no blood here which leads us to believe that the deceased was murdered somewhere else and dumped here," she explained.

"Any idea about time of death?" Moore interjected.

The coroner studied the victim's hands and lips for a moment. "Less than 24 hours."

"Okay. We'll let you get along with your work. We're heading back to Put-in-Bay," Ohlemacher said as he led Moore away. "Crime of passion," he mentioned in a solemn tone.

"Why do you say that?"

"Murderers in a rage over a lover or spouse will typically kill with a knife because it's more personalized than shooting someone with a gun," Ohlemacher explained.

"Which makes Spider the prime suspect," Moore proposed as they soon reached the boat and started untying the lines.

"Exactly."

"I don't understand why he would have turned on Riley if they had plotted together to kill Elke and run off with the life insurance money," Moore protested. "Unless Spider decided not to share the insurance money."

"But Spider would lose out on extra cash flow," Ohlemacher said as he guided the boat away from the island.

"How's that?" Moore asked.

"Net proceeds from the sale of Riley's house, unless it was heavily mortgaged. We'll have to do more checking."

"Right."

"All supposition, Emerson. But we will get to the root of this."

"Are we going to visit Spider?"

"Yes. I have a few more questions for him."

They returned to the dock at the Miller Marina where they

each picked up their vehicles. Moore followed Ohlemacher to Spider's place where they parked in front of the B&B. The men then walked onto the porch and knocked on the screen door.

"I'm coming," Spider yelled from the back of the first floor.

"Did you smell that?" Moore asked as the two stepped away from the screen door.

"Yes. Bleach," Ohlemacher answered all-knowingly.

"Cleans up blood, right?" Moore postulated.

"And it can destroy any DNA. We'll check it out." Ohlemacher said quietly.

The door opened and Spider emerged. He seemed very calm.

"Busy?" Ohlemacher asked.

"I'm always busy. What can I do for you?" he growled.

"Have you seen Riley Bostle in the last twenty-four hours?"

"Yes. What about it?" he asked, perturbed at the intrusive question.

"She's been murdered," Ohlemacher said slowly as he closely watched Spider's reaction.

"What?" Spider asked as the blood drained from his face. "Riley is dead?" Spider reeled in disbelief. He looked away, then looked back. "That can't be!" He dropped onto one of the porch chairs as Ohlemacher and Moore watched his body shudder for a few moments.

"Are you okay? Do you want me to go inside and get you a glass of water?" Ohlemacher offered. He was eager for an opportunity to see where the bleach scent originated.

Spider responded quickly. "No. You don't need to go inside. I'm fine."

"If you don't mind, tell us about your visit with Riley?" the chief requested.

"Sure. She stopped by last night. She came over to offer her condolences for Elke," Spider said as he regained control of his emotions and became more like his old self.

"How long did she stay?"

"Over three hours."

"That's a long time to offer condolences," Moore suggested.

Spider ignored Moore.

"What happened during that period of time?" Ohlemacher probed as he began asking a series of questions.

"Nothing. We just talked."

"What about?"

"Primarily about Elke."

"What else?"

"Just usual stuff. Why?"

"This is standard questioning, Spider. Which room were you in?"

"The kitchen."

"What time did she leave?"

"I don't know."

"What do you mean you don't know?"

"We had a disagreement. I blew my top and I left."

"What time was that?"

"Around 11:15."

Ohlemacher made an entry in his notebook. "Where did you go?"

"I went for a walk."

"Anybody see you on your walk?"

"Yes. People driving by on their golf carts or in their cars."

"Anyone you could give us a name for?"

"Hey, what are you getting at? Do you think I killed Riley?" Spider snarled angrily.

"We're not drawing any conclusions, Spider. We are just

gathering facts and trying to figure out what happened to Riley," the chief responded.

"I didn't have anything to do with her death," Spider steamed as his anger threatened to erupt. "I think I'm finished with answering your questions, and I'm calling my lawyer."

"One more thing and we'll leave," Ohlemacher added.

"What's that?" Spider thundered.

"Do you mind if we take a peek at your kitchen?"

As his inner inferno erupted, Spider jumped to his feet. "If you want to go through my house, you better have a search warrant. I'm done," he raged as he opened the door and stormed inside, locking the door behind him.

"That was interesting," Moore commented as he and Ohlemacher walked down the steps to the sidewalk on Delaware Avenue.

"Very."

"He certainly appeared shocked to hear about Riley's death," Moore suggested.

"Yes. He's either a very good actor or he really was shocked by the news."

"If he was acting, he did a much better job than when we told him about Elke's death."

"I noticed that, too," Ohlemacher agreed.

"Did you notice how he didn't ask how she was killed or where her body was found?"

"It might have been due to the shock. Sometimes people don't think straight when they are in that state."

"I don't know if that man would ever think straight. What do you think about his story?" Moore asked.

"I'm not sure what to think. I can't imagine that he didn't see somebody who he knew while he was on his walk."

"What's next?"

"We need to get a search warrant," Ohlemacher said as he headed for his car. "You coming?"

"No, unless you need me."

"Not now. It will take me a while to get a search warrant. We'll talk in the morning."

"Okay. Since I'm here, I'll pay a visit to my aunt," Moore explained as he walked over to the Doorbell Inn. Knocking on the door, he waited.

"Anne, we've got company. Your nephew is here," Ada said as she opened the door, allowing Moore to enter.

"Hello, Emerson," Aunt Anne greeted Moore as she walked into the front room. "Anything new on Elke's murder that you can tell us?"

"Not really. It's an ongoing investigation," he explained as a disappointed Ada walked out of the room.

She returned with a plateful of fudge. "Help yourself. We just made it."

Moore looked at the chocolate fudge and took one piece. "Hmmm," he said after biting into a piece.

"Got any extra?" a voice squeaked from the screen door.

They turned around and saw Cranston peering through the screen.

Moore looked at Ada who nodded for him to open the door. "You arrived just in time," Moore said as he opened the door and introduced the ladies to the police officer.

"That's what my instinct does for me. It has me show up at just the right time," Cranston boasted as he took two pieces and gobbled them down. He smacked his lips as he reached for two more. "These are delicious."

"What brings you down here, A.C.?" Moore asked.

"I was wrapping up my patrol and saw Uncle Tom's car parked here with yours. But, it looks like he left before I could finish a run out to the airport."

Moore nodded. "He's back at the station if you want to find him."

"I probably should go and see if I can help him since we have another murder," he said self-importantly.

"Another murder?" Aunt Anne exclaimed in horror.

"What? Did I hear you right?" Ada grilled Cranston.

Moore wrinkled his brows with disgust at Cranston's lack of professional discretion.

"Riley Bostle. Didn't Emerson tell you? He and the chief were on the scene. I heard it on the police radio," Cranston continued.

"We just saw her yesterday. Isn't that right Anne?" Ada stuttered with shock.

"You did?" Moore jumped in to ask.

"Yes. We were sitting on the porch and she walked by on the sidewalk. She went next door to visit Spider," Ada answered.

"Did you see her leave?" Moore probed.

"No. You might want to ask Henry," Ada suggested.

While they were talking, Cranston walked over to the bird cage. "What's the name of your little buzzard?" he asked as his attention was distracted.

"Beak-a-doo," Ada replied.

Cranston bent over and began teasing the bird by holding his piece of fudge just outside of what he thought was its reach. He was wrong as the bird pecked him.

"Ouch," he yelled as he recoiled from the bird's attack. Its sharp beak had struck Cranston's finger, which was now bleeding. "Hey you little pecker! I'm going to take you to Uncle Tommy's house and feed you to his cats," he lectured the bird.

"You leave my bird alone," Ada said as she stepped between Cranston and the bird cage.

Cranston stuffed the rest of the fudge in his mouth. "I guess I'll get back to official police business. Someone needs to look out for the safety of the islanders since we have a serial murderer on the loose," Cranston cracked as he walked out the screen door.

He stopped on the porch steps to examine his finger and was pleased to see that the bleeding had stopped. He looked down the street toward the chamber office for any traffic violators, then swung his gaze over to the public beach. That's when he saw Hawkins' overturned grocery cart.

Littering ordinance violation, Cranston smiled as he strode down the stairs and walked toward the beach.

Meanwhile Aunt Anne asked Moore, "Do we have to be concerned about a serial killer?" She was aghast with fear.

"No. There's no evidence of that," he reassured her. Turning to Ada, he asked, "Where's Henry?"

"He's out back in the garage. Follow me. You can go out through the kitchen," Ada suggested.

"Thanks. I'd like to talk to Henry," Moore said as he followed her.

She busied herself at the kitchen sink as Moore exited the inn and walked to the garage. He could see Henry through the open garage door. He was working at his workbench.

"Henry, can I interrupt you?"

Startled, Henry looked up and saw Moore. "Sure Emerson. What's up?" he asked meekly.

"I wondered if I could ask you a couple of questions regarding Elke's disappearance."

"I'd be glad to help in any way."

"Good. This actually relates to last night. Were you home all evening?"

With a confused look on his face, Henry nodded. "Yes. I didn't go anywhere."

"Were you outside or inside?"

"I was sitting on the patio until 11:00, then I went inside."

Moore pointed to the rear of the Spider's Web. "Did you hear an argument or notice anything unusual at Spider's place?"

"Yes. There was a big ruckus just before I went inside the house. It sounded like Spider arguing with a woman."

"Did you recognize the woman's voice?"

"No."

"Could it have been Riley Bostle?"

"I don't know her well enough to say. You know there's a big rumor that he was having an affair with her," Henry proudly disclosed.

"I heard something along those lines."

Henry continued, "That rumor has been around for some time."

"Anything else you noticed or heard?"

Henry thought a moment. "I do remember that all of the yelling stopped after I heard a door slam."

"Did you happen to notice if Spider walked out of the house?"

"No. I was on the patio, and it sounded like it might have been a front door."

"Anything else?"

"No."

Moore's eyes were drawn to a display of knives in a collector's case, mounted on the wall. The door to the case looked askew and there was an open space in the middle of the knife display.

"You collect knives, Henry?" Moore asked.

"I do. I had a pretty good collection until someone broke in last night and stole my pride and joy. It was a 10-inch, handmade, steel hunting knife with a deer antler handle. My great-great-grandfather carried it during the Civil War."

"I'm sorry to hear that. Any idea who stole it?" Moore pressed as he thought about the knife wounds in Riley's back.

"No. I don't lock the garage. Anyone who knows I collect knives could have broken in." Henry added, "I'm fixing a new lock for the case."

"If you think of anything else that I should know, please give me a call," Moore said.

"I'll do that," Henry assured him.

Moore walked out of the garage and was halfway down the driveway when he heard his name called. He turned to see Henry walking toward him.

"I just remembered something."

"What's that?"

"I heard Spider's boat start last night. We had the bedroom window open and I heard it. Its motor is a bit noisy."

Moore's attention was riveted on Henry. "Do you know what time that was?"

"Yes. Because I looked at the clock next to my bed. It was 2:00 a.m."

"Did you hear any voices?"

"No."

"Did you hear the boat return?"

"No. I was out like a light."

"What about Ada? Did she hear anything?"

"No way. That woman could sleep through a tornado!" he exclaimed. "And if you wake her up for anything, she gets as mad as a box of frogs."

"Could you check with her and Aunt Anne, then let me know if they did hear anything?" Moore asked.

"Be glad to, Emerson," Henry replied. As Moore turned to resume his walk to his car, he saw Cranston hurrying toward him. Cranston's face reflected haughty pride.

"Emerson! Emerson!" he called breathlessly. "You guys should have had me involved in your murder investigation from the get-go. I found another body," he announced with a sense of self-importance.

"Where?"

"The beach. It's Rio Hawkins," he said as they started for the beach. "Looks like somebody stabbed him in the back."

Moore was stunned by the news.

"Are you sure it's Rio?" Moore asked as they headed for the public beach.

"Absolutely," Cranston confirmed proudly.

"Are there any footprints around him?" Moore asked as they began walking on the boardwalk that was surrounded by sea grass.

"Other than mine, no. I did walk over and check his pulse. There wasn't any. It looks like the killer brushed away any footprints with a branch. The branch is over there," Cranston reported as he pointed to the discarded branch.

"Did you call Tom?"

"Of course. He should be here momentarily," Cranston said as he surveyed the beach.

Moore studied the body which was face down with its hands outstretched. "What's that?" he asked as he kneeled on the edge of the walk.

Cranston looked to where Moore was pointing. Scratched in the sand at Rio's fingertip was a letter. It was a "W".

"I guess that solves the case. Rio's dying action was to tell us who murdered him. It was Spider White," Cranston concluded proudly.

"Maybe," Moore said, careful not to jump to conclusions.

"Come on Emerson. You don't want to give me credit for cracking this case. You've never worked with a professional like me before," Cranston babbled pompously.

Moore heard a vehicle stop at the end of Delaware Avenue. He stood and saw the chief. Before he could greet him, Cranston announced again, "I found Rio. I solved the case, Uncle Tommy."

Ohlemacher nodded his head as he walked down the wooden walk and bent down to look at Rio's body. "No one disturbed the crime scene, right?" he asked.

"Other than A.C. checking for a pulse," Moore answered.

Ohlemacher stood and allowed his eyes to sweep the area. "I called the forensic team and coroner to come back out. They should be here within the hour," he said as he looked at the dwindling daylight.

"A.C., I want you to go back to the station and bring us four of the portable lights. We need to light up this area so we can search for clues."

"I'm on it," Cranston said as he scurried to his vehicle and drove away.

"While we're waiting Tom, I should update you on what I learned from Henry Hoover," Moore suggested.

When he concluded his update, Ohlemacher responded, "Interesting. Knife disappears. We have two deaths by a knife within twenty-four hours. Maybe one occurred in Spider's kitchen because we smelled bleach. Spider's boat goes out in the middle of the night. Maybe Rio here saw something that he shouldn't have seen and he was caught watching. Then he's stabbed."

"And we have the clue left by Rio that points to Spider White," Moore offered.

"The 'W'," Ohlemacher affirmed. "You have to like it when the victim reveals who the murderer is."

"I'll say."

"Are we going to arrest Spider tonight?" Moore asked.

"We'll do it in the morning. I should have the search warrant by then and I want to get an initial read on what the forensic team discovers."

When Cranston returned, they moved quickly to set up the portable floodlights and worked with the coroner and forensic team when they arrived.

Unnoticed to them was the figure peering through the curtains of the Spider Web's front room. It was Spider White and he was watching with interest as events unfolded.

CHAPTER 19

Next Day, Early Hours
Warren's Museum

The buzzing of his cell phone awoke Moore out of a deep slumber. It had been a long previous day and he was dog-tired. He looked at the caller ID and a burst of energy surged through him when he saw the name Aunt Anne. She never called him in the middle of the night.

"Is everything okay?" he asked as he answered the phone. He was leaning on his side and noted the time was 3:00 a.m.

"Spider's house is on fire, Emerson. Henry called the fire department. They should be here shortly. I'm worried that it will catch Ada's inn on fire," she ranted emotionally.

"Get out of the house and stand across the street. Be sure that Henry and Ada are with you," Moore instructed as he jumped out of bed and threw on a pair of shorts and his shoes.

"Henry went out back to try to put it out with the garden hose," she said.

Moore had her on his speaker phone as he was getting dressed and raced out of Warren's house. "Let's not worry about Henry," Moore said as he jumped in his car and sped away. "You and Ada get across the street right away, understand? I'm on my way and will be there in a few minutes."

"Okay," she said as they ended the call.

Moore immediately phoned Ohlemacher. "Tom, did you hear that Spider's place is on fire?"

"Yes. I'm on my way."

"See you there," Moore said as he headed to town. When he turned onto Delaware Avenue, he saw the fire department had arrived with two pumpers, a tanker and a ladder truck. Firefighters were hurrying in dragging hoses and hooking up to the nearby fire hydrant.

Moore pulled to the side, parking next to the street. He quickly left the car and darted down the street to where he found his aunt and Ada watching the burning B&B next door.

"Are you both okay?" he asked hurriedly as he surveyed the activity, looking for Spider.

"We're fine," Aunt Anne assured Moore.

"Henry's out back, fighting the fire," Ada said proudly.

"Good. Anyone seen Spider?"

Both women shook their heads negatively.

"What about guests? Do you know if they had any guests and if they made it out safely?" Moore asked.

"Spider hasn't had any guests since Labor Day," Ada said as Ohlemacher arrived in his car, parked and joined them.

"No one has seen Spider," Moore called as he and Ohlemacher hurried toward Assistant Fire Chief Mark Wilhelm. The gray-haired leader was coordinating his team in attacking the fire.

"Anybody spot Spider? Did he get out?" Ohlemacher asked Wilhelm.

Barely taking time to answer, Wilhelm replied, "Not yet, Tom. I'll let you know. You can check the boat dock and the apartment."

"Mark, in case you didn't know, Ada said that there were no guests staying at Spider's," Moore volunteered.

"Thanks," Wilhelm replied. He turned back to focusing on the fire.

Ohlemacher and Moore walked over to the lake side of the

house. They saw Braxton watching the fire from the far side of his apartment. Before they could walk over, they heard Cranston's voice.

"Good thing I was down here on patrol," he called as he walked over to join them.

"You called this in?" Moore asked in disbelief.

"Yep. Called Uncle Tommy and the fire department. I turned around at the end of the street. That's when I saw the smoke and flames," he boasted with self-aggrandizement.

"Did you see Spider?" Moore asked.

"No. I used my patrol car's speaker and yelled fire. I think I woke up half of South Bass Island. I put on my siren and left the car. I ran to the kitchen door, but it was locked. Then I ran around back and yelled toward Spider's bedroom, but I didn't get any reaction. I saw the lights go on at Ada's, then saw Henry come out."

"Where's Henry now?" Ohlemacher asked.

"The last I saw him was by his garage. He had watered it down and was hosing the side of Spider's place."

"A.C., did you wake Braxton?" Moore asked.

"I think my siren did. He came out in his pajamas and has been standing over there watching the flames."

"Let's go talk to him," Ohlemacher suggested.

The three men walked over to where Braxton was standing.

"Are you okay?" Ohlemacher asked.

"Other than a headache that I got from your officer's siren blasting, I'm fine. I was in a deep sleep. This looks terrible," he said as the flames reflected red on his face.

"Have you seen Spider?" Ohlemacher asked.

"No. When I came out, none of the lights were on in his house," Braxton explained. "I saw your officer run around, knocking on the door and calling his name. I don't know. Maybe he's not home," Braxton suggested.

"What's that over there?" Cranston asked excitedly as he pointed to the side of the apartment wall.

They all turned and saw Cranston pointing at two five-gallon gas cans.

"Are those yours?" Ohlemacher asked Braxton in a serious tone.

"No. And I don't recall seeing any gas cans being stored there," Braxton replied defensively with a look of surprise.

"Uncle Tom, there's two empty bleach containers here, too," Cranston said proudly.

"Empty?" the chief asked.

"Yeah. I kicked both of them over," Cranston explained.

"I don't know anything about any of this stuff," Braxton fretted.

Ohlemacher closely observed Braxton's reaction. "When did you last see Spider?"

"I don't know. Maybe a day or two ago." Braxton's face appeared concerned. "Listen, I didn't have anything to do with this if that's what you're thinking."

"How about this? Did you have anything to do with this?" Cranston asked with haughty pride.

The three men looked at Cranston who had walked over to the gas cans. He was carefully holding what looked like a hunting knife. His face was beaming at his discovery.

"I don't know anything about that. It's not mine," Braxton stated firmly.

"Where did you find the knife, A.C.?" Ohlemacher asked as the men walked over to him.

"It was on the ground between the gas cans and the wall."

"I've heard about the murders, and they were committed by someone with a knife. It wasn't me. I don't know anything about this," Braxton said as despair seemed to sweep over him.

Ohlemacher pulled an evidence bag out of his pocket and instructed A.C. to place the knife inside it. Turning next to Braxton, Ohlemacher added, "I trust that you're not planning on leaving the island any time soon."

"No. I don't have any reason to run from this. I'm innocent," Braxton moaned nervously.

"Not a word to anyone about this knife. You three understand?" Ohlemacher ordered.

They nodded their heads in agreement.

"We'll have the forensic team look for fingerprints on this and the handles of the two gas cans and bleach containers. A.C."

"Yes?"

"I want you to go over and tell Mark Wilhelm about the two gas cans. That might help them with their investigation for the cause of the fire."

"Okay, Uncle Tommy." Cranston walked over to Wilhelm who was helping his team set up floodlights, directed at the house.

Ohlemacher turned his attention back to Braxton. "Brock, have you seen anything unusual around here the last couple of days?"

Braxton laughed nervously. "Everything around this place is unusual."

"Seriously," Ohlemacher pressed.

"Nothing that I can recall."

"Let me know if you do," he said as Cranston returned. "A.C., I want you to take this knife and those two gas cans and bleach containers back to the station. Be careful that you don't smudge any fingerprints on the cans," he cautioned. "Wear gloves."

"Right Uncle Tommy," Cranston said as he hurried away.

The chief and Moore walked away from Braxton.

"What do you think?" Moore asked in a hushed tone.

"Finding that evidence was too easy. I think all of that was planted. I don't believe that Braxton would be so stupid as to place the knife and cans there."

"Unless he really wants to use a little reverse psychology on us," Moore ventured.

"I don't know. We'll see what the fingerprints show us."

"Too bad this fire happened before we could go in with a search warrant," Moore lamented.

"Now that is suspicious. Someone doesn't want us snooping around that kitchen. I'm betting that Riley was killed there," Ohlemacher surmised.

"You think Spider set the fire and tried to frame Braxton, then got off the island?"

"Could be the first two. But I have a hunch that he's still on the island," Ohlemacher said as he nodded toward the Lyman boat hanging from the hoist. "Besides, I don't think he'd leave behind his pride and joy."

"What a long day and night this has been," Moore offered.

"That my friend is an understatement. Riley's dead. Rio is dead. Elke, of course. And now Spider's house is on fire! Incredible!" the exasperated chief recapped.

Moore and Ohlemacher stood silently over the next hour as the firefighters worked quickly to extinguish the flames. Most of the damage appeared to have been isolated to the rear of the structure where the kitchen, office and master bedroom were located.

Once the fire was out, the firefighters carefully entered the house and began a room-to-room search. Wilhelm and another firefighter cautiously entered through the now destroyed kitchen door. Ten minutes later, Wilhelm emerged. When he spotted Ohlemacher, he walked over to him.

"We were able to contain the fire to the rear of the structure. Most of the damage was done in the addition. The kitchen is where accelerants likely were used to start the fire," the savvy Wilhelm explained. "We'll know more for sure once the fire investigation is completed."

"Gasoline?" Moore asked.

"Probably, since you spotted those cans," Wilhelm said. "There's additional damage done to the office and less fire damage to the master bedroom. The rest of the house incurred smoke and water damage."

"Any sign of Spider?" Ohlemacher asked Wilhelm.

"I was just coming to that, Tom. We found his partially burned body in his bed. Henry Hoover didn't realize that streaming water on that side of house went through the open bedroom window and kept Spider's body from being charred."

"He die of smoke inhalation?" Moore probed.

"No. Stab wounds is my guess," Wilhelm suggested.

"What?" Moore asked incredulously.

Ohlemacher shook his head in disbelief. Another murder! Multiple homicides on these Lake Erie western basin islands were far from the norm.

He immediately began walking toward the B&B to go view the body. "Is it safe for me to enter now, as we likely have another homicide to investigate?" Ohlemacher asked Wilhelm.

"I'll get you a couple of fire hats to wear. I don't want to take a chance of something dropping from overhead on you," Wilhelm said as he radioed one of his team to bring them over.

After Moore and Ohlemacher placed the protective hats on their heads, the three men entered the B&B.

Ohlemacher stood next to and viewed Spider's body. Moore and Wilhelm each stood outside the bedroom so as to limit any potential added impact to what was an apparent crime scene. The chief observed that Spider was laying on his back with what appeared to be knife wounds in his chest. He was naked. His shoes and clothes were on the floor next to the bed.

"Angry lover?" Moore whispered to Wilhelm.

"If it was, I don't want to meet her," Wilhelm cracked.

Ohlemacher took several pictures with his cell phone camera before they left.

"So where does this leave us?" Moore asked Ohlemacher.

"Maybe Spider killed Elke, Riley and Rio, then, for some reason, he was killed. Or maybe Spider didn't kill anyone. Somebody else did and tried to blame Spider," Ohlemacher answered thoughtfully.

"What about Rio writing the 'W' in the sand?" Moore challenged.

"That's perplexing. I have to believe Rio wrote it. He had sand under his fingernails if you looked closely," the chief explained.

"I missed that," Moore admitted. "Then there's the evidence pointing to Braxton," he added.

"That's intriguing. Was Braxton in on this from the get-go and we missed it? Or did someone else kill Elke and Riley? Then a second party took out Spider and set the fire? Is someone trying to frame Braxton? This is getting more complicated," Ohlemacher said.

"I'll say," Moore agreed.

"It's going to be interesting to see whose fingerprints are on the knife, gas cans and bleach containers," Ohlemacher ventured. "Let's check in on your aunt and Ada."

"Yes. We should," Moore agreed as he and Ohlemacher walked next door to find the two women had returned to the front porch.

"Quite a bit of excitement," Ohlemacher announced as he climbed the steps to the porch.

"Oh my. I'll say, Tom," Ada remarked.

"We're lucky that the fire didn't jump over here," Aunt Anne added.

"Mark and the team did an incredible job in keeping it contained." Looking around, Ohlemacher asked, "Where's Henry?"

"He's still out back," Ada replied.

"Let's check in with him. You ladies seem fine," Ohlemacher said as he turned to go locate Henry.

"With all of this excitement, I'm not sure that I'll be able to get back to sleep," Aunt Anne offered.

"I know what you mean," Moore said as he smiled at his aunt. He began to follow the chief down the steps toward the back yard.

They found Henry winding up his garden hose.

"It's been a busy night," Ohlemacher stated as he looked at Henry, partly covered in soot and smelling like smoke.

"You betcha," Henry replied with a confident smile. "But I was able to wet down my garage and the side of our house before I turned my hose on Spider's house." He adjusted his glasses and asked, "Was Spider home?"

Ohlemacher nodded. "Yes, but he didn't make it." He didn't

explain any farther since he wanted to keep that information close to the vest.

"Sorry to hear that. He wasn't as mean as people said. Just would go on a rampage from time to time," Henry added.

"Henry, do you have a picture of that knife that you're missing?"

"Sure. Come on inside," Henry said as he walked inside the garage. He opened a drawer under his workbench and shuffled through some files. "Here's one," he said as he held up a picture.

After reviewing the photo, Moore and Ohlemacher gazed at each other with an all-knowing look. It appeared similar to the knife they had found next to Braxton's apartment.

"Let me take a picture of that," Ohlemacher said as he pulled out his cell phone and snapped away.

"You want to take this one? I probably have a couple of other pictures of it," Henry volunteered.

"No. That's okay. You keep it."

"Could I see that picture?" Moore asked. When Henry handed it to Moore, Moore grabbed Henry's hand and lifted it to his nose. "What's that I smell, Henry?"

"Probably gasoline."

The chief stared at Henry's hand as he was surprised by the revelation.

Henry pointed to his lawn mower which was on its side. Next to it was a small shallow pan. "I was working on my mower last night and I washed out a couple of the parts in gasoline. It's hard to get rid of that smell on your hands," Henry explained nervously. "Do you know what I mean?"

"I do," Moore said as he paused to see if Henry would comment about gasoline being used to set the fire next door. Neither Ohlemacher or Moore had mentioned gasoline being used to start the fire.

When Henry put the knife picture away and didn't comment, Ohlemacher asked, "Henry, did Brock Braxton visit you often?"

"Once in a while. I told him that he could borrow any of my tools if he needed them. Just to leave me a note what he was taking."

"Did he ever borrow any of your knives?" Moore asked as he looked at the glass cabinet on the wall that displayed the knives.

"No. Never. He liked looking at them, but never held one."

"You ever notice anything strange about Braxton?" Ohlemacher asked. "How did he interact with Spider or Elke?"

"Not really. Spider liked to yell at him, so he kept his distance. Elke seemed to dote on him. He's a good-looking guy. A lot of women like to dote on Brock," Henry observed.

"Do you have any reason to believe that Brock and Spider were having an affair?"

A shocked look crossed Henry's face. "Absolutely no way. As I said, Spider's hobby was yelling at Brock. And Brock was a real ladies' man."

"How about Elke and Brock having an affair?" Moore quizzed Henry.

"I wouldn't be surprised. She was a looker. I'd see her go into Brock's apartment at times."

"When he was home? Maybe she was just checking on the apartment?" Moore asked.

"Oh, Brock was home alright. Spider noticed what was going on, too. I could hear Spider chewing her out through that open window when she came back inside." Henry pointed at the window to Spider's office. "They would really get into it.

And she got the worst of it."

"How about Rio Hawkins?" Ohlemacher asked.

"He did his best to keep a low profile. That guy was not only homeless, but he was harmless. He'd stop by and help me with projects when he needed a little pocket change."

"Thanks Henry. Let me know if you think of anything that could help our investigation," Ohlemacher said as he and Moore began to walk away.

"You can count on it," Henry added as he followed them out, turning off the garage light.

Moore and the chief walked to the front of the house where they saw the firefighters winding up their hoses. The ladder truck was pulling away as it returned to the fire station.

"I think we should call it a night, Emerson," Ohlemacher sighed.

"Tired?" Moore asked.

"Yes. It has been long 24 hours."

"It has. I'll get in touch with you later this morning and we can sift through everything," Moore suggested.

"You read my mind."

The two men departed for their homes.

Moore parked his car at Warren's home and walked inside to his bedroom. He stripped off his t-shirt and shorts, then dropped into his bed. He was bone-tired from the deadly discoveries of the last 24 hours. Sunrise would arrive shortly and much too soon.

He felt like a horse run to the ground. His brain was on a sprint, tumbling out of control with replays of the recent tragedies. He knew that he needed to rest, but he couldn't stop the treadmill of ideas his mind was creating. While the rest of the island was embracing dreams and peaceful rest, his brain churned overtime in trying to determine the murderer's identity. What had they overlooked?

When he did fall asleep, it was fitful with him tossing and turning. Several times, his eyes darted to the clock on the bedstand, adding to his frustration about not getting his rest. He needed a clear mind for that coming day's investigation.

Mixed with his tussle of conflicting thoughts were nightmares involving a zombie-like Spider entering his bedroom with dervish-like movements and stabbing Moore over and over. He couldn't get the image of Spider, dead on his bed, out of his mind.

CHAPTER 20

**Later The Same Morning
Warren's Museum**

The sound of Moore's alarm was, in many ways, a welcome relief. He shut it off and sat up on the edge of his bed. He glanced at the alarm clock and saw it was 9:00 a.m. He was still tired. Stretching, he stood and slipped on a robe, then grabbed his shaving kit. He walked slowly downstairs on his way to the bathroom.

"You were up late," Warren greeted Moore from where he was working on the engine of his Model T Ford.

"Tough night," Moore replied.

"I'd say it was worse than that with the fire and Spider's death on top of Riley Bostle and Rio Hawkins getting themselves killed," he commented with a sly grin.

"I guess word got around," Moore offered, a bit miffed.

"You have to remember this is a small island, Emerson. People talk and try to look out for each other, especially if we've got a serial murderer on the loose. Any ideas who it is? That Brock Braxton seems likely to be the culprit," Warren said as he answered part of his own question.

"We're still investigating. Tom doesn't want us to make any comments."

"How's your aunt? And the Hoovers? Any fire damage to their place?" He peppered Moore with questions.

"They are all okay. I'm going to pay them a visit after I clean up and have breakfast."

Warren studied Moore for a moment. "You really look

tired, Emerson."

Moore chuckled. "That is an understatement," he said as he headed for the bathroom.

"There's fresh coffee in the kitchen when you're ready."

"Thanks, Richard," Moore said as he walked into the bathroom, pulling the door closed behind him.

Forty minutes later, Moore parked his car in front of the Doorbell Inn. He stepped out and surveyed the inn for any damage, but didn't see any. He did note that the windows were open and saw several fans at work. Must be trying to get rid of the smoke smell, he thought as he walked up the steps to the porch. He glanced next door at the damage to the Spider's Web B&B as he took the steps.

"You look tired, Emerson," Moore's aunt greeted him from the front porch where she was enjoying a cup of coffee.

"I didn't sleep well."

"I don't think any of us did, dear. There's coffee inside if you want to grab a cup. Ada is upstairs cleaning and Henry is out back."

"Thanks," Moore said as he walked inside. A couple of minutes later, he walked out with a cup of hot coffee. He sat in a chair next to his aunt and took a big sip of the tasty brew.

"You didn't see anyone inside when you were getting your coffee, right?" she asked as she leaned toward him.

"No. Why?"

Aunt Anne began to whisper to him. "Word got around that Spider is dead. You should have seen the look of excitement on the faces of these two – Ada and Henry."

Moore wrinkled his brow, not understanding what she was getting at. "Why were they excited?"

"They were talking about buying the Spider's Web and how

they would fix it up. They were like two kids in a candy store," she said with a conspiratorial look on her face.

Moore sat back as he processed her news. Could it be that Ada and Henry had a deadly scheme to buy the house and part of it included eliminating anyone involved with owning it? Moore wondered quietly. He would have to let Ohlemacher know his aunt's revelation.

What if Ada and Henry had committed the murders of Elke, Riley and Rio, used the bleach to clean the kitchen, murdered Spider, started the fire and tried to frame Braxton? What if? What if? Moore's mind filled with the possibilities.

Ada and Henry were in the prime location to do all of this without attracting attention to themselves. How convenient!

"Did you hear anything else?" he asked in a low voice.

"No," she replied. Suddenly her face changed to an expression of surprise. "You don't think that they are behind all of these murders, do you?" she asked with shock.

"I don't know, but you can't let on that we had this discussion or suspect anything. One, we don't want to falsely accuse them. Two, we have to get more facts," Moore spoke quickly, then drained his coffee cup. His exhaustion was replaced by a rush of adrenaline at the news.

"I'm going to go out back for a second and talk to Henry," he said as he stood and walked down the steps. "Not a word," he cautioned his aunt before walking around the inn.

When he arrived at the back, he discovered Henry seated on the patio and speaking with the housekeeper, Marie Donley.

"Hello Henry. Hello Marie," Moore greeted the two as he walked over and sat in an empty chair.

Henry acted like he had been caught with his hand in a cookie jar. "We were just talking about the fire," he sputtered awkwardly.

"Yeah. Now I'm out of one of my jobs," Donley complained.

Moore was surprised by her reaction. He expected to see some remorse at the news of Spider's death.

"You still have our place," Henry reacted.

"But we're in the off-season now. You won't have enough work for me to even come close to making up what I was making before. I don't know how I'm going to make it financially. I'll have to find something else here. I don't know. Maybe I'll head to the mainland and find work," Donley moaned.

With her being present, Moore decided to ask her a few questions to see if she could shed any light on the police investigation.

"Marie, I don't know how we overlooked you. I forgot that you worked next door as a housekeeper."

"That's the story of my life. No one cares about poor old me," she whined.

Moore ignored her comment and asked, "You're aware of the murders?"

"Of course, I am. Where do you think I've been? Antarctica?" she fumed.

"No. You've been around Elke and Spider. Do you have any idea who might have killed them?" Moore probed.

"Brock Braxton," she replied without hesitation.

"Why do you say that?"

"He and Spider didn't get along."

"Why didn't they?"

"Spider thought Brock was having an affair with Elke."

"Was she?"

"I think so."

"Why do you think so?"

"She spent enough time in his apartment. I'm sure she wasn't reading him fairy tales," Donley cracked.

"I understand why you think Braxton killed Spider, but why kill Elke?"

"Lovers' quarrel gone bad. That's my guess," she pronounced.

"What about Riley Bostle then? Why would Brock kill her?"

"I don't know. Maybe she saw something that she shouldn't have?"

"Like what?"

"I don't know."

"What about Rio?"

"Same as Riley."

"You're missing something, Marie," Henry spoke up with pride.

"What, Henry?" Donley twisted in her chair and gave Henry a death stare. She didn't appreciate him intruding on her exchange with Moore.

"Brock doesn't know how to operate a boat. He couldn't have taken Elke's or Riley's body over to Middle Bass Island to dump them," Henry said as he shifted uncomfortably.

"But you do, Henry, and that's your boat right next to Spider's," she countered, still miffed.

"Now wait a second. I had nothing to do with any of that," Henry protested.

Turning back to Moore, Donley continued. "Besides, I heard that you found gasoline cans next to Brock's apartment. That should tell you who did in Spider and set the fire."

"And bleach containers," Moore added. He was always surprised how fast the island grapevine passed along information.

Henry's eyes widened at Moore's comment about the bleach

containers.

"Hey! I bet Brock stole the bleach containers from Spider's place. If you find my fingerprints or Marie's on one of them, it was because she ran out of bleach and borrowed a container full from our place," Henry explained defensively.

"Thanks for letting me know, Henry." Moore stared at Donley as he drilled in just a little deeper. "Marie, why did you need bleach?"

"There was something spilled on the kitchen floor and I didn't have enough bleach to clean it up. So, I borrowed some from Henry," she clarified defensively.

Moore didn't respond. He used his silence as a tool to see if she would say anything else. The silence worked as Donley took the bait.

Changing the topic, she said, "Besides, Brock stole Henry's knife. You found it next to the cans, right?"

Moore was stunned that she knew about the knife. Only Ohlemacher, Cranston, Braxton and he knew about it unless one of them leaked it to the island grapevine.

"What do you know about a knife?" Moore probed.

"Nothing other than what I heard people talking about this morning at the Island Market," she answered.

Moore's mind was working overtime as it processed the information from the morning's discussion. He realized he had better call Ohlemacher.

"Well, I should be going," he said as he stood. "Thank you both for your time."

"Any time Emerson," Henry replied.

Donley said nothing. She appeared distraught about Moore's line of questioning. Her face was like stone as she stared at the back fence. She was perturbed at possibly being thought a murderer suspect.

Moore walked down the driveway. As he reached for his cell phone to call Ohlemacher an idea struck his mind like a thunderbolt. He walked over to his car and leaned against it as he called the chief.

"Hello Emerson," Ohlemacher answered.

"Boy, do I have some news for you," Moore started.

"Before you begin, Mark Wilhelm called me. He spent some time earlier this morning, trying to determine how the fire started. It's arson. He thinks someone doused the kitchen floor and Spider's bedroom with gasoline. Then he or she balanced a lighted cigarette over a paper cup full of gasoline. When the cigarette dropped into the cup, it started the blaze. Doing it that way gave the arsonist time to get away."

"That's interesting. I think I have a new suspect," Moore said eagerly.

"Tell me."

Moore related the conversations with his aunt, Henry and Donley.

"You think Ada and Henry are behind all of this because they wanted to own the Spider's Web?" Ohlemacher questioned.

"Could be, but Marie Donley just soared to the top of my list of suspects," Moore added.

"Yeah, funny how she knew about the knife and gas cans," Ohlemacher remarked.

"She did say she heard islanders talking about it at the Island Market this morning," Moore offered.

"That's good to know. My nephew probably leaked the information after we agreed to keep it confidential. He just loves to brag about what he knows. I'll have to talk to him about that. Interesting thought about Ada and Henry being behind all of this," Ohlemacher commented.

Then Moore dropped a bombshell.

"Tom, what if we misread the clue that Rio left for us?"

"What do you mean?"

"Rather than Rio writing a 'W' in the sand, what if it was a 'M' and we were looking at it from the wrong direction?"

"Could be, but who is the 'M'?" Ohlemacher asked.

"Marie Donley."

Ohlemacher nodded at the revelation. "It sure does point to her, doesn't it? We haven't considered her at all."

"We haven't. I think she's done a pretty good job flying under the radar the entire time," Moore suggested.

"Hang on a minute. I want to check one thing."

Moore waited while Ohlemacher put him on hold.

When the chief returned, he reported, "I just checked with my nephew to be sure he didn't say anything to anyone about the knife. He didn't. I'm coming over to question Marie. While you're waiting, I want you to go next door and ask Braxton if he said anything to anybody about the knife."

"Okay. I'll do it right away."

The two men ended the call.

Twelve minutes later, Ohlemacher parked his car in the Doorbell Inn driveway. As he stepped out, he was greeted by Moore.

"I talked to Brock. He didn't say anything to anyone about the knife. The poor guy is a bundle of nerves," Moore reported.

"Good. I'm glad that you came over to the car before we go out back to talk to Marie." Ohlemacher looked around before proceeding. "Is your aunt inside?"

"No. She and Ada left a couple of minutes ago. They said they were going to the Island Market," Moore answered.

"What about Henry? Do you know where he is?"

"As far as I know, he's still out back, talking with Marie. Why?"

"There's more to Marie than what we knew. I ran a quick check on her before I left. She spent several years in a psychiatric hospital in Cincinnati. She pleaded guilty to second-degree murder for the stabbing death of her boyfriend, but entered a second plea of innocent by reason of insanity," he explained quietly as he looked around.

"Wow. I didn't have a clue," a stunned Moore commented.

"None of us did, Emerson. One more thing, she was caught on the Ohio River when she took his boat out to dump his body."

"So, she knows how to operate a boat!" Moore exclaimed.

"Apparently," Ohlemacher ventured. "I bet she was here on the island, trying to get her life together."

"You think she had a thing for Spider and killed off Elke and Riley because they were in the way?"

"Maybe. Then rejected by Spider, stabbed him," Ohlemacher conjectured. "We want to be very careful how we approach her," he cautioned.

"I'm with you on that."

"Let me take the lead in questioning her," he said as the two walked toward the back of the inn. They spotted Henry and Marie standing in the garage at Henry's workbench.

"Hello Marie, Henry," Ohlemacher said as he and Moore walked through the garage door opening.

"Hi Tom." Henry had a perplexed look on his face at seeing the chief while Donley seemed to shrink back. "What can I do for you?"

"It's not so much you Henry, as it's Marie," Ohlemacher

began.

"What do you want with me?" she asked suspiciously.

"Marie. I wanted to ask you a couple of questions."

"I answered Emerson's questions a few minutes ago. Why are you asking me questions?" she squirmed.

"Just some follow-up. That's all."

Donley nodded for Ohlemacher to continue as she lowered her eyes and stared at the garage floor.

"Do you know anything about the deaths of Elke, Riley or Rio?"

"Nothing more than what I've heard around the island," she responded warily.

"What about Spider's death?"

"Nothing. I was there yesterday afternoon to do some of my basic housekeeping duties. I may have been there for 45 minutes," she offered without hesitation.

"Was Spider home?"

"Yes."

"What was he like?"

"He seemed normal."

"Describe normal," Ohlemacher pushed as Moore closely scrutinized her reactions.

"You know. He can be abrupt. Snap at you," she said as she shrugged her shoulders nervously.

"Snap at you?" Henry interrupted. "He sounded like a screaming banshee. I could hear him hollering at you over here."

Donley's face paled at the revelation. "It wasn't that bad."

"I don't know about that. You certainly were giving it back to him full throttle. I didn't know you could yell so loud!" Henry added.

Donley's eyes narrowed as she gave Henry a death stare.

"What were you arguing about?" Ohlemacher asked.

"My pay," she answered unconvincingly as she also recalled the questions that Moore had asked her about the bleach and the knife. She felt pressure building like a noose being tightened around her neck.

Ohlemacher cocked his head in disbelief. "Marie, I think it was something more than that," he surmised. Then he poked hard. "Did Spider want to break off the affair you two were having?"

Donley couldn't control her reaction as Ohlemacher pushed the right button with his relentless style of questioning. Her face went pale. Her brain stuttered for one moment, wrestling with the emotional scars from her past as it overloaded and crashed. Logical thinking went out the window, replaced by an eruption of pure fury as she lost control of the angry feelings that she had fought to keep below the surface. The underdeveloped prefrontal cortex of her brain allowed her violent temper to explode as she broke.

"He betrayed me," she spat the words out with vengeance. "I did everything for him. I killed Elke for him when he asked me to pick her up behind the Overboard. He was going to get off scot-free from a murder charge and then he's going to run off with that whore, Riley. Well, I took care of her. And when Rio saw me, I sliced him up, too," she confessed wild-eyed.

Her appearance seemed to transform demon-like as her inner rage spewed out in torrents. Her chest was heaving.

"Why kill Spider? Wouldn't he run off with you?" Ohlemacher pushed.

"Spider betrayed me," she repeated. "He held me close while he plunged an emotional knife into my heart and whispered sweet nothings. I found an envelope. It had a ticket to

Brazil that he printed out. He was going to leave me."

"So, you killed him?"

"Not right away. I had my revenge. I took him in the bedroom for one last time. He had no idea what I had in store for him," she laughed cruelly. "When I was finished with him, I really finished him," she cackled. "I used the knife I stole from Henry!" she declared.

Using a stabbing motion, she brought her hand down repeatedly as she demonstrated what she had done. "He fell asleep. Over and over. I stabbed him! The first was in the heart!" she roared with rage.

"Then I watched him bleed out. At first, the blood flowed thick and strong, then it slowed as his pulse weakened. His skin became gray." Her eyes glowed with evil glee as she recanted the event.

Moore was astonished by how she enjoyed reliving the moment. She was a real mental case, he thought.

"I dipped my finger in his blood and wrote the word 'betrayed' on his forehead," she smirked with an evil smile.

Ohlemacher looked at Moore. They had seen the word written in blood on Spider's forehead, as did Wilhelm, but had kept it among themselves.

"Marie Donley, I'm arresting you for the murders of Spider White, Elke White, Riley Bostle and Rio Hawkins. Anything you say . . ."

"No, you're not, Tom!" she shrieked as she grabbed a knife from the open display cabinet and held it to Henry's throat as she stepped behind him. "You'll do no such thing or I'll kill Henry. You know I won't hesitate. I'm good with a knife," she chortled in a deadly tone.

Moore started to edge toward her, but Ohlemacher grabbed

his arm. "Don't," he cautioned Moore.

"What's the next step, Marie? You know that this has to end one way or another," Ohlemacher declared.

"It's going to end my way, Tom," she cracked defiantly. "Tom, I want you to slowly take your weapon out of your holster and, with your left hand, put it here on the workbench next to me."

Ohlemacher did as he was instructed, placing his Glock .40-calber semi-automatic pistol on the workbench, then stepping back.

"We're all going to take a little walk to the boat dock. You two walk in front of Henry and me. If you try anything, I'll slit Henry's throat," she warned. Then, for effect, she tightened the knife and broke the skin, allowing a trickle of blood to emerge.

"Okay. We'll do as you say," Ohlemacher said as he and Moore turned and began walking to the dock. They didn't see her put the knife down and pick up the Glock or the extra set of keys to Spider's Lyman that Henry had. She kept one hand on Henry's shoulder as she walked behind him with the gun barrel against his back.

"You don't have to do this, Marie," Ohlemacher said as they walked.

"Shut up and keep walking," she said in a deadly tone.

When they reached the dock, she instructed Moore, "Emerson, I want you to lower the Lyman into the water. Tom, give me your handcuffs."

Ohlemacher handed her his handcuffs, and she placed one cuff around Ohlemacher's wrist. She pulled the other cuff through two aluminum support brackets and cuffed Henry's wrist. The two men would not be able to escape.

While she was busy, Moore had lowered the Lyman as she

directed. While her back was turned, Moore saw his chance to escape. He quietly ran toward the back side of Spider's fence.

When Donley turned around, she saw him dodge behind the fence and swore. "There's nothing he can do!" she boasted as she jumped in the Lyman and started its engine with a roar.

The boat sped away, rounding Chapman's Point. Soon it was around East Point and heading for Middle Bass Island.

Hearing the boat depart, Moore returned to the dock. "Do you have an extra set of keys for the cuffs, Tom? I'll free you."

"No. I'll radio in for someone to come out here and free us. Take my hideaway .38 pistol. It's in my ankle holster and go after her in Henry's boat. Henry, where are the keys?"

Moore bent down and withdrew the .38 from Ohlemacher's ankle holster.

"They're in my right front pocket and I can't reach them. Emerson, you're going to have to reach in my pocket," Henry whined.

A look of trepidation crossed Moore's face. "Henry, I don't want to reach into your pants pocket."

"I wouldn't either, Emerson. But you're wasting time," Ohlemacher said in a serious tone. "I don't want her to get away."

Throwing caution and dignity to the wind, Moore reached in carefully and withdrew the keys. He turned to the boat hoist and quickly lowered Henry's Robalo R200 into the water.

"Where do you think she's headed?" Moore asked as he jumped aboard and started it.

"Canada, probably. Get going. I'll get a call into the Coast Guard and get them in the hunt. Don't waste any time. You have the best chance of catching her!"

Moore shoved the throttle forward as he started to pursue

Donley. As he rounded East Point, he spotted the Lyman to the east of Middle Bass Island. It wasn't heading for Canada; it was entering Schoolhouse Bay. Moore set his course to catch her.

When Moore entered the bay, he spotted the Lyman. It had been run aground on the rocky shoreline in front of the airport runway. As he neared the shore, he saw Donley talking to Eddie Sheller next to his plane.

Moore was astonished. Was Sheller, after all, her accomplice? What was the link between the two of them? A myriad of thoughts raced through Moore's mind.

Moore ran Henry's boat up on the rocky shore. He was pleased to see that Cranston apparently had pulled over Dave Nostrant's truck near the shoreline on Deist Road next to Hauncks Pond. Moore then hurried to Cranston's vehicle as he glanced to see Sheller and Donley climbing into the plane.

"Hello Emerson. Rough way to dock a boat," Nostrant greeted the approaching Moore.

Before Moore could say anything, Cranston piped up, "Checking up on me, Emerson? I caught Dave driving left of center. He's getting a ticket," Cranston beamed.

"Don't have time to explain. I need your car. Radio Tom that Marie Donley is on that plane," Moore yelled as he jumped into the police car. He was glad that the engine was running as he shifted it in gear and spun the vehicle around. In seconds, he was rocketing down the nearby runway to block the plane that had started to take off.

Moore pointed the car at the oncoming aircraft. He could see the look of surprise on Sheller's face, then caught Donley shoving the barrel of the Glock to the side of Sheller's head.

Next, Sheller knocked the weapon away and began to struggle with Donley. As they fought, the plane gathered speed and veered to the left. It departed the runway through a recently tree-cleared area and crossed Deist Road before plummeting nose first into the 30-foot-deep water of Hauncks Pond. In seconds, only her tail remained above water.

Moore turned sharply to his right and barreled to the pond where he brought the police car to an abrupt stop. He ran out of the car to the water's edge. Nostrant and Cranston hurried over from the adjacent roadway as Moore stripped off his shirt and kicked off his shoes.

"I'm going to try to rescue them."

"There's Eddie," Nostrant said as Sheller's head broke the surface of the water.

"Are you okay?" Moore called as Sheller swam to the shore.

"I'm fine. I tried to help Marie, but she was thrown out the other door. Did she surface?"

"If you mean that body floating on the other side of the tail, the answer is yes," Cranston cracked as he walked along the shore to get a better view.

Moore dove into the pond and swam to her body. He turned it over so that her face was up and began swimming her to shore. Her skin color was pale and she wasn't breathing as Nostrant and Sheller helped pull her body onto the shore.

Moore joined them and started to give mouth-to-mouth resuscitation as the men gathered around. After five minutes, Moore stopped. "She's not responding. I think she's gone."

"Looks like she's got a big bruise on her noggin," Cranston volunteered as he looked closely.

"There's nothing you can do," Sheller agreed.

"Too late," Nostrant concurred.

"A.C., can you radio Tom and tell him what happened here?" Moore asked.

"Sure," Cranston replied, reaching for his radio as he walked a short distance away.

Moore turned to Sheller. "You okay, Eddie?"

"Yes, but I don't know what all that was about."

Moore eyed Sheller suspiciously. "What was she doing in your plane? Were you two flying off somewhere together?"

Sheller's eyes narrowed at the insinuation. He didn't like Moore's tone. "I don't know what's going on here or what you're thinking, Emerson. The lady calls me and told me that she had to charter my plane right away due to a family emergency.

"I hurried to meet her at my plane. She panics when she sees you and pulls a gun on me when I told her I was going to abort taking off. We fought over the gun and crash my plane into the pond. And I get the stink eye from you for trying to help someone?" Sheller was upset.

"Sorry Eddie. I should have known better," Moore apologized before explaining what had transpired since confronting Donley at the Doorbell Inn.

"That's why she was in such a big hurry to leave. She said she needed to get to her father's place in Grand Rapids right away. I didn't know I was going to help her escape," Sheller added.

"No problem," Moore surmised as he looked at the body. "I guess this case is closed."

"Hey guys. Look what I found on the edge of the pond," Cranston yelled as he approached the men. He was holding something in his hand. "I found me a blue bullfrog. I've never seen anything like it before."

The three men shared a look of grave concern.

Moore was the first to speak. "A.C., the blue bullfrog is

poisonous. They secrete poison from their skin."

Next Emerson Moore Adventure:
Rainbow's End
20th Anniversary Edition